the

bear

went

over

the

mountain

books by william kotzwinkle

william kotzwinkle

doubleday

new york

london

toronto

sydney

auckland

the

bear

went

over

the

mountain

PUBLISHED BY DOUBLEDAY
a division of Bantam Doubleday Dell
Publishing Group, Inc.
1540 Broadway, New York, New York 10036

DOUBLEDAY and the portrayal of an anchor with a
dolphin are trademarks of Doubleday, a division of Bantam
Doubleday Dell Publishing Group, Inc.

This novel is a work of fiction. Names, characters, places,
and incidents either are the product of the author's
imagination or are used fictitiously. Any resemblance to
actual persons, living or dead, events, or locales is entirely
coincidental.

book design by jennifer ann daddio
frontispiece by kate brennan hall

Library of Congress Cataloging-in-Publication Data

Kotzwinkle, William.
    The bear went over the mountain : a novel /
William Kotzwinkle.
        p.   cm.
      1. Authors and publishers—United States—Fiction.
    2. Bears—United States—Fiction.   I. Title.
    PS3561.O85B43   1996
    813'.54—dc20   96-2296
                                                       CIP

All Rights Reserved
Printed in the United States of America
October 1996
First Edition
10 9 8 7 6 5 4 3 2

with thanks to bronson platner

The bear went over the mountain
The bear went over the mountain
The bear went over the mountain
to see what he could see . . .

the

bear

went

over

the

mountain

A fire raged in an old farmhouse. The indifferent flames were feeding on the pages of a manuscript. It was a novel called *Destiny and Desire* and its pages curled up at the edges one by one, then flared into light and turned to smoke.

The farmhouse burned quickly. The beams and rafters collapsed into a fiery pile, and when the unsuspecting owner returned, all that was left of his house, and his novel, was a smoking hole in the ground.

The farmhouse had been the sabbatical hideaway of Arthur Bramhall, an American literature professor at the University of Maine. He was ill suited to teaching, as he was subject to depression, and preferred being alone, knowing he was poor company when he was depressed, which was most of the time. He'd purchased the old farm in hopes of having sex with women who'd also moved to the country and might themselves be depressed. Most of these women looked depressed to him, or at least angry, probably about having to live in the country. His plan was that after having sex with them, he'd write a best-selling novel about it. He'd written the novel, but it'd been from his imagination not his experience, for he'd found that women who'd moved to the country wore shapeless overalls, frequently smelled of kerosene, attended solstice festivals, and refused to shave their legs; he thought of them as fur-bearing women, which tended to depress his libido. Consequently, the only excitement he'd had was his house burning down.

Now he stood in the darkness of the winter night with the embers of his disintegrating house lighting his face. Jutting out from the embers were the twisted shapes of his metal file cabinets, his gooseneck lamp, and his typewriter. He paced along the edge of the hole, looking for traces of charred paper. Bright little tongues of flame licked up at him, cautioning him to keep his distance until they were through. He knelt at the edge of the smoking hole and mourned his lost book.

"I understand that Bramhall has built himself a little cabin with his insurance money," said Bernard Wheelock, a brilliant young lecturer in American literature at the University of Maine.

"Yes, he's rewriting his book," said Alfred Settlemire, a full professor at the same institution. Settlemire was a distinguished-looking figure with a high handsome forehead and a leonine head of hair, accented by a carefully shaped goatee on his prominent chin.

"It was terrible, his book burning in the fire," said Wheelock. "What a blow for a guy who tends to look on the dark side."

"Well, was it actually terrible?" asked Settlemire. "I'm sorry his house burned down, but as for his book—it was a deliberate steal of *Don't, Mr. Drummond.* He told me so himself. He studied all the best-sellers and thought that was the one he could copy."

"Not an easy task," said Wheelock, who'd tried it himself.

"Well, but is that why one takes a sabbatical? To copy a best-seller? Successfully or unsuccessfully? Is that, one asks oneself, why one writes?" Dr. Settlemire used the word *one* a lot. He himself had published a book that traced the use of simile in Robert Frost and among other things it showed that Frost had used the word *like* as a simile .54 times per page. That was the sort of work that meant something. Work of commitment, one felt.

"Have you read any of Bramhall's book?" asked Wheelock.

Settlemire let out a snort of contempt. "Before the fire, he sent a few chapters to me for comment, which of course one couldn't really give him, as one didn't know where to begin. His heroine is making a go of a run-down farm she's inherited. She smells of kerosene but is lovely anyhow."

"Sounds like it might be interesting."

Settlemire stroked his excellent goatee. "One knows farms. Studying Frost, one must. The farm in Bramhall's book is a pipe dream."

"Poor Bramhall."

"It'll never be published. One is quite certain of that."

In his little cabin, Arthur Bramhall rewrote his book. He did not bother to have his telephone line reconnected, and he saw no one except an old lumberjack who lived on the next ridge and occasionally dropped by to chat. Aside from this, Bramhall had no interruptions. The fire had taught him something, about patience, renewal, fortitude. He gave up trying to write a copy of a best-seller and wrote in a fever of inspiration straight from the heart—about love and longing, and loss, and about the forces of nature, into whose power he'd been initiated. By the last page of the book, his new heroine was glowing with an inner radiance gained from being humbled by nature. There was still lots of sex, but it had a connection to the ancient moods of the forests, to crow songs, and fox cries, and the crackling of a fire in the hearth.

"I've written the truth," said Bramhall as he closed the manuscript and patted it tenderly. In the pit of destroying darkness where his lifelong depression had its seat, he'd lit a tiny lamp of cheer. "Tomorrow you go out into the world," he said to his manuscript.

He put it in a briefcase and carried it with him out of the house. "I'm going to buy a bottle of champagne for us," he said to his briefcase. A problem for city dwellers who move to the country is that they have no one to talk to but the septic field, or in this case, their briefcase.

He went across the meadow, far from his cabin, and carefully laid the briefcase under the boughs of an old spruce. The boughs hung to the ground and the manuscript was completely hidden. "If there's another fire, you'll still be safe."

He smoothed out the edges of the pine boughs as he'd done every day for the past few months and smiled with satisfaction at his hiding place.

A bear watched Bramhall from a spot a few hundred yards away. Like Bramhall, the bear was a decent, hardworking sort. He followed his own regular rounds, from the stream where he caught trout and salmon, to the abandoned orchards where he ate apples in the fall, to the mountainside where he gorged on blueberries in summer. He was good-natured, and always hungry. He'd recently broken into the kitchen of a restaurant and eaten all the pies and cakes and then the ice cream and chocolate sauce and a can of colored sprinkles. The tastes and smells of these items haunted him; the balminess of spring seemed to carry them on the air, torturing him. The man had left something valuable under the tree. Maybe it was a pie.

The bear liked to roll in meadows and wave his paws in the air. He ate garbage when it was available and enjoyed rummaging at the dump for pizza boxes with splashes of cheese and other delicacies in them. He lived for his stomach and once a year at the first sign of summer had astounding sex. He was wise to the ways of the forest and crafty when it came to the ways of man; when he'd forced the window of the restaurant, a look of extreme concentration had come into his beady eyes, not unlike the look Arthur Bramhall had while seated at his typewriter.

Now, as Bramhall got into his car and drove off to buy champagne, the bear padded across the field and slipped under the branches of the pine tree. He approached the briefcase cautiously and sniffed at it. There was no trace of pie. Still, it paid to be thorough. He put his teeth around the handle of the briefcase and carried it deeper into the woods. When he felt secure, he set the briefcase down and whacked it several times. The latches popped and the briefcase opened. He sniffed disappointedly at the manuscript. Termite food, he said to himself, and turned to go, but a line on the first page caught his eye and he read a little ways. His reading habits had been confined to the labels on jam jars and cans of colored sprinkles, but something in the manuscript compelled him to read further. "Why," he said to himself, "this isn't bad at all." There was lots of sex and a good bit of fishing, whose details he thought were accurate and evocative. "This book has everything," he concluded. He slipped the manuscript back into the briefcase, clamped the handle in his teeth, and headed toward town.

While his manuscript was being stolen by a bear, Arthur Bramhall was having coffee with a fur-bearing woman. They were in a diner on Main Street in the small town to which they went each week to do their food shopping. "I finished my book," he said to her, and she said, "Well, that's exciting."

"Yes, I suppose it is," he said, attempting to maintain his urbanity though he was secretly bubbling with happiness. If his book succeeded, he'd never have to return from his sabbatical. He'd never have to see the English department again, nor be tempted to eat greasy pizza in the student union building, where his English students sat around reading comic books featuring space Amazons clad in aluminum foil.

"I'm sure it's going to be a success," said the fur-bearing woman kindly, although she'd written him off her serious-relationship list. He had a sturdy build and a pleasing head of wavy brown hair; his brown eyes were gentle, and he had a nice smile, but her sort of man had to smell of pine sap and woodsmoke and the great outdoors, as she did. Arthur Bramhall could never be trained up to any sort of satisfactory level. For one thing, he ironed his jeans.

"It's nice running into you," he said. While it was true that he ironed his jeans, he was a decent human being with much natural affection for other people. But because he was shy and introverted, he'd never found a lasting relationship with a woman, and in his loneliness he tended toward moods in which he stared out of his window like a goldfish. Right now he was in the manic phase of his cycle. "What've you been doing with yourself?" he asked with genuine interest.

"Oh, I'm still doing my wellness work," said the fur-bearing woman with a dubious grasp on English but a firm hold on economics. For fifty-five dollars she gave her clients what she called an energy massage. Bramhall had paid her fifty-five dollars only to discover that her hands never touched his body, only swept the air above it with a dyed-purple chicken feather. He pretended to feel much better after this because he liked to encourage others in their work. Now he listened to the fur-bearing woman's latest insights into energy fields, auras, magnetized water, and tried to find her attractive, despite the smell of kerosene. He tried to think of her as resembling the heroine of his book, but the sensually stimulating properties of kerosene worked better on paper than over coffee at the local diner. She said, "You know that the earth is coming into a feminine cycle, don't you?"

"I'm sorry, I didn't know that."

"Yes, the feminine force is getting stronger every day. I'm organizing a moon goddess festival to celebrate it."

Bramhall nodded. The fur-bearing woman loved festivals. On nights when he was only mildly depressed he could help himself get out of it by thinking how wonderful it was that he wasn't at a moon goddess festival.

The fur-bearing woman took his hand in hers. "Close your eyes," she said, "and concentrate on success through Jupiter, the planet of good fortune." The fur-bearing woman was a decent human being too, who sincerely believed she helped others with her purple chicken feather.

Bramhall closed his eyes, and thought again of his briefcase, under the tree. He thought of it the way a Bushman thinks of his carved fetish wrapped in bat skin.

"I see very good things happening with your book," said the fur-bearing woman. "I see someone taking it."

Bramhall felt an effervescent thrill in his abdomen, as if he'd swallowed the Antacid of Happiness. With his eyes closed, he realized she had an understanding voice, and he felt her good will toward him. She was a fruitcake, but so were the other fur-bearing women of Maine. The winters were too long for them, and it drove them into peculiar activities. He hoped his little novel might comfort them. Its hero was a renegade archaeologist looking for fossils in Maine; he too had been humbled by nature and had learned to respect it, and to respect women, for they were the crown of nature. Bramhall thought that the fur-bearing women who read it could believe, for a little while, that the hero had come to *their* run-down farm to respectfully poke around in their fossils.

The bare overhead bulbs of the diner were reflected in the quartz crystal the fur-bearing woman was wearing on a chain around her neck, and it seemed to reflect her isolation as well. He suspected she was as lonely as he. He imagined himself taking her home, running her a hot bath, and leaving a shaving brush and razor conspicuously on the edge of the tub. "I think you might like my book," he said shyly.

She nodded in agreement. "I have the very strong feeling that there's an angel watching out for your book right now."

The bear waited at the edge of town until nightfall. As the town was in rural Maine, there was only one clothing store, but the bear wasn't fussy. He forced a back window and went in. Going through back windows usually led to shoveling down the sweets, but he forced himself to put thoughts of food aside as he prowled the darkened aisles of the store. A display mannequin caused him to draw back cautiously, but his nose quickly ascertained that the human-looking figure was made of wood. He approached the dummy and carefully studied the items of clothing it wore. Then he went and collected those same items in the store, choosing a suit of the kind lumberjacks wear to funerals. He worked himself into a shirt without too much trouble, but fastening the buttons was difficult. He got a few of them through the little holes and called it good enough. After several tries he got himself into the pants. They were on backward, as he hadn't entirely grasped the nature of the garment. "Not a bad fit at all," he remarked as he gazed at his shadowy reflection in the mirror at the back of the store. He slipped into the suit jacket and returned to the store dummy for a quick comparison. The painted eyes of the dummy seemed critical. "A tie, of course," said the bear, and found one with hula dancers on it. His taste was deplorable but he was only a bear. Studying the knot at the dummy's throat, he fashioned his own. "That looks good," he said, though the knot was unusual. He added a baseball cap and shoes, went to the cash register and emptied it, then climbed back out the window. As he hit the pavement, he shook the sleeves of his coat and balanced himself in the upright position. "It's remarkable what a suit can do for a bear," he said.

He walked slowly and clumsily, his shoes unlaced. The briefcase handle was in his teeth and this drew the attention of several passersby. They said nothing, but the bear noticed their superior smiles. What could it be? he wondered. He caught a glimpse of himself in a window and stopped. "Something wrong there," he said to himself as he studied his reflection. Baseball cap is on straight, and the suit looks fine. His small, gleaming eyes stared back at him. Briefcase in the mouth!

Sheepishly, he transferred it to his paw. The old habits are going to die hard, he said to himself as he walked on.

Later, seated in the back row of the diner on Main Street, he opened the briefcase again and examined the title page of the manuscript.

DESTINY AND DESIRE
BY
Arthur Bramhall

Title's fine, thought the bear to himself, but I don't see myself as Arthur Bramhall. No, that name wants changing. Something snappier. It'll come to me.

On the table before him was coffee, toast, and two little pyramids of jam and half-and-half containers. He ran his gaze over the containers thoughtfully.

Jam

Perfect name, you can't do better than Jam. Now for a first name.

Again his eyes ran over the labels on the containers.

Half-and-Half Jam

Very distinguished.

Or is it too ethnic?

With his paw, he blocked out some of the lettering on the half-and-half container.

Half Jam

Sounds too Nordic. But I feel I'm close. Let me just . . . a slight modification . . .

With the tip of his shiny claw, he covered up the *f* in *Half*.

That's a name that will mean something to people.

There was a pen in the briefcase, and a few blank

sheets of paper. With great concentration, he laboriously
wrote a new title page:

DESTINY AND DESIRE
BY
HAL JAM

Arthur Bramhall returned home that night and went across the field with a flashlight to retrieve his manuscript from beneath its tree. At first he thought he had the wrong tree. He ran from tree to tree, yanking back branches and shining his flashlight on the ground.

"No," he cried, "no, no."

He stared through the trees at the cold, pitiless moon rising through the branches, the moon of thieves and crossroads. He fell on his knees and beat his fists on the ground. Then he got up and ran through the fields screaming, "It's gone! It's gone!" He shook his fist at the trees and shouted, "Why? Why did you do this to me again?" When he came to his senses, he sought the help of Vinal Pinette, the old lumberjack who lived nearby. Vinal Pinette came and investigated the scene under the tree.

"Bear."

"What?"

"A bear's got 'er."

"A bear's got my briefcase?"

The old lumberjack pointed to faint indentations in the ground. "Tracks are right there."

"Well, let's follow him!"

"A bear travels fast when he wants to. Could be in the next county by now."

Arthur Bramhall fell back against the trunk of the tree. He'd already spent what little resilience he had. Years of depression and uncertainty had plundered him, and now a bear had finished him. "My life is over."

"Had valuables in that suitcase?"

"My novel." Bramhall stared at Vinal Pinette. Much as he liked the old man, he knew Pinette couldn't grasp the significance of what had been lost.

"We kin go after him," said Pinette, "but I don't think it'll amount to much. They al'uz say—if the bear sees you, you won't see the bear."

"Yes," said Bramhall woodenly, not wishing to cause any more inconvenience to his neighbor. He stumbled back through the field, his brain mixing up that killer cocktail he knew so well, the one that was going to result in him feeling like a corroded anchor at the bottom of the sea.

"It's a marvelous book," said Chum Boykins of the Boykins Literary Agency, "but of course I don't have to tell you that."

The bear nodded, and Chum Boykins smiled, tapping his finger on the face of the manuscript. "What I like best is how *fresh* it is. At the same time, it has a haunting familiarity, of something we've never fully appreciated."

The bear nodded again, modestly. His pants were no longer on backward, and his confidence was growing. Outside the office windows was the buzz of the great hive of humanity; its frenzied activity was difficult to fathom, but he soothed himself with candy bars, several of which were in his pockets right now.

"I've got an editor in mind," said Boykins. "Do you know Elliot Gadson at Cavendish Press? I think he's our man. He's got the clout, he's the right age, and this is the kind of book he loves. I'm going to call him and get the wheels in motion."

Boykins pressed his intercom. "Margaret, get Elliot Gadson for me, would you, please?"

He turned back to the bear. "Elliot knows I only call him when I've got something special. Do you want coffee?"

"Sugar," growled the bear, carefully pronouncing the most important word in his limited vocabulary.

"Margaret, bring us a coffee, would you, please, lots of sugar. Thanks." Boykins smiled at the bear. "Anybody ever tell you how much you resemble Hemingway?"

"Who?"

"Yes, who indeed. I think you just might be the one to make people forget him."

"Pie," said the bear to the waiter at the French restaurant to which Boykins had taken him.

"Nothing else?" asked Boykins.

"Cake ice cream."

"It's nice to see someone who's not obsessed about their weight."

"Winter," said the bear, patting his stomach.

"Yes, it *was* a difficult winter." Boykins's eyes were dark, their gaze intense. His gestures were precise. He leaned forward, supporting his chin with thumb and forefinger. "Have you got anybody representing you on the West Coast? A Hollywood agent? Because the cinematic possibilities for your book are very strong. I can just see that huge solstice bonfire on the big screen."

Boykins moved the vase on the table a few inches to

the right. Yes, he said to himself, that's better. Boykins had spent his childhood performing numberless compulsive rituals; in the middle of the night his parents would find him standing bolt upright in his room, the coils of compulsion holding him paralyzed.

"In fact, the whole book reads like a movie, which I'm sure isn't news to you. It's a brilliant piece of crossover work." He smoothed the edge of the tablecloth down, several times. As a child, Boykins had no time for sport, no time for girls, no time for anything but smoothing his pillow hundreds of times, then standing on one leg in the bedroom, arms raised for hours in supplication to the faceless power that ruled him. "I've started working with a wonderful young woman at Creative Management. I'm sure you'd get along with her very well."

The bear wanted to be careful about those he got involved with. "She like pie?"

"Pie?"

"Yes."

"Well," laughed Boykins, "I'm sure she likes it. Whether she eats much of it, I can't say." Boykins crunched a piece of celery in his strong jaws and chewed it thirty-seven times. While standing bolt upright in his college dormitory the night before graduation, and clicking his fingers thirty-seven times, he'd wondered how he could ever fit into the normal world with such an affliction. "I can tell you this, Zou Zou Sharr is one of the smartest women in Hollywood. And she's beautiful, for whatever that's worth. She knows the important directors, she knows the stars, and she's a tough negotiator. And just so *you* know it," smiled Boykins, "so am I." Brutal negotiations were nothing to a man who'd spent his youth and young manhood standing on one leg. Who could back him down? In spite of his savage negotiating, publishers liked him. When they took on a writer represented by Boykins, they knew Boykins would edit text, design jackets, write ad copy, invent publicity gimmicks, drum up the sales force, call reviewers, court the media, and woo bookstores. His quiet insanity drove him to seek control over everything and it paid off in sales. "I don't like to use the word *trendy*, Hal, but I think your book definitely touches a contemporary nerve."

The bear sniffed, enjoying the weave of perfumes and colognes in the air, which made him feel as if he were in a field of flowers. He sipped some wine. His only previous experience of alcohol was a bottle of cooking sherry he'd downed while rampaging in the kitchen of that rural Maine restaurant; its effect had been blurred by the great number of pies that'd accompanied its ingestion. Now the effect was more noticeable and his sensitivity to the fragrant air increased. His nose, which for years had led his instincts, led him now, without deliberation, without preliminary weighing of what was at stake. He slid out of his chair and down onto the floor of the restaurant, where he rolled around with his paws in the air as a bear will do when he finds a field of flowers that fills him with happiness.

Boykins went rigid in his chair. His client was making an ass of himself. On the other hand, to roll off your chair and writhe ecstatically on the floor in the middle of lunch showed remarkable freedom from constraint. Boykins, bolt upright in body and soul, saw in Hal Jam the image of what he'd never been, a happy child at play in the dream of life. Boykins stared in fascination.

The headwaiter was not fascinated. He charged over, outraged at this breach of etiquette in his elegant domain.

The bear twisted back and forth, using the accepted bear maneuver of raising arms and legs to get momentum into the twist and thus scratch more thoroughly and more deeply. His eyes were half-slitted with ecstasy. The face of the headwaiter was indistinct, but the waiter's mustache, and his whining voice, had the semblance of a weasel.

"Monsieur, please, not during lunch!"

Bears don't like their good times interrupted by impertinent weasels. The bear's paw shot out. The headwaiter had spent a lifetime dodging through swinging doors. He ducked and the blow sailed past the tip of his mustache.

Boykins dropped to one knee beside his client, first making sure that his knee landed precisely in the center of one of the carpet's rectangular patterns. "Hal, I think you're drunk."

The bear froze, aware of many pairs of eyes on him.

I'm getting a feeling here, he said to himself. Possible blunder?

He quickly flopped onto his stomach, pushed himself upright, and took his seat with as much dignity as he could muster, which was considerable, owing to a life of undisputed primacy in the forest.

The headwaiter had a similar authority in the room he ruled, and was equally skilled in the restoration of dignity, aided by Boykins quickly slipping him a twenty.

Boykins lifted the wine bottle. "I've seen too many writers ruin themselves on this stuff, Hal. And you don't need it. You're the real thing already."

The voice of Boykins blended with the other human voices in the room, becoming the sound of bees. "Bees honey," said the bear, his elbow sliding forward on the table.

He's fried to the eyebrows, thought Boykins.

"Honey life," said the bear, fighting to create easy conversation, but he could feel people's glances and their superior smiles. They spoke their thoughts effortlessly, while his moved ponderously. His agent was looking at him anxiously, with no idea of what he was trying to say about honey. And he himself didn't know. I'm floundering, he said to himself. Panic shot through him, and his eyes darted back and forth.

"Well," said Boykins, trying to return to the orderly procession of business matters, "how do you feel about publicity?"

The question broke apart into pieces and the bear couldn't fit the pieces together. His long tongue ran nervously over his snout. A woman who'd just joined a party of Tempo Oil executives at an adjacent table noticed the bear and kept her eyes fastened on him as the voices of her male colleagues broke dully around her. Now, there, she thought as the bear's red velvet tongue slipped over his nose again, is a man.

"The sales force will insist on a tour," said Boykins, "if we get the kind of money I'll be going after."

The bear had lost the thread to which he'd managed to cling from Maine to Manhattan. The buzz of the restaurant was an unbearable judgment on his animality. He slapped his paws over his ears.

"I understand, Hal, you don't want to hear about it yet. You've just written a novel and it's precious to you. But these days the author is as much the product as the book."

The racing stream of human speech glistened as it curved around obstacles and glided on, relentless in its gradient, while he panted in animal stupidity.

And then his nose twitched, the olfactory bulb at its

24

root a thousand times more sensitive than that of a human. He straightened and moved his head around to isolate the natural scent he'd found within the synthetic veil of perfumes. There it was, moist, cool. "Salmon."

"Yes, they do it skewered with tomatoes, mushrooms, and green peppers."

"Raw," said the bear with a resurgence of primal authority.

"Raw?"

"Raw female. Lots of eggs. In my teeth." The bear tapped at his incisors.

My god, thought Boykins, he *is* another Hemingway.

Arthur Bramhall stared at the blank sheet of paper in his typewriter. He had no words, no thoughts, no inspiration. This time the forces of nature had broken him. He rested his head on the space bar. "I should have used a computer. Everything would be on floppy disk. But I was afraid of all the power failures in the boondocks. I said, if a typewriter was good enough for Hemingway, it's good enough for me. What a tragic conceit."

He lifted his head. Beside him on the desk was a mug from the University of Maine, with its emblem—a black bear—painted on the side. He picked it up and put it away in a drawer. Then he stared out the window of his office toward the tree under which he'd left his briefcase. He strained to see beyond it, into the woods, hoping for the sight of a real black bear lumbering by with a briefcase, but the only sight was Vinal Pinette strolling down the lane. Bramhall got up from his desk as the old lumberjack entered the cabin. "Why did he take it, Vinal?" asked Bramhall. "What use would a bear have for a briefcase?"

"Bears are funny creatures," said Vinal

Pinette. "I had one steal a shirt of mine off the clothesline. Gave it an awful thrashing and then throwed it aside. Something about that shirt he didn't like, I suppose, and he got worked up about it."

"I feel as if I'm dying," Bramhall admitted, hoping that by some miracle Pinette would have words of wisdom for him, gleaned from long years of country living. He had put a character like Pinette in *Destiny and Desire,* an old backwoods philosopher who entered at crucial moments like this and saved the day with his hard-won natural wisdom.

"I used to feel just the same," said Pinette. "Felt that way every year in spring when the timber company airplane sprayed us with DDT. It knocked the spots right out of me. The timber folks said it was the very best stuff in the world, and I don't doubt it was, I just didn't seem to take to it." Then, looking into Bramhall's sagging countenance, Pinette said, "But what I always say is if you ain't got a noseful of porcupine quills, you're doing okay."

Bramhall put his face in his hands. "How can I go back to the University of Maine and face my colleagues?"

"They pay good wages up to the college, do they?" Like most country people, Vinal Pinette took a great interest in wages earned in exotic places.

"I don't want their wages. I want freedom."

"Arf McArdle used to talk about freedom too. Had a wife, eleven kids, and a mother-in-law who was as tough as a steel-toed boot. One day the mother-in-law sent him to the store for some soap, and nobody ever saw him again. Something about that request for soap set Arf on course for parts unknown."

Bramhall gazed out the window again, toward huge fleecy clouds moving slowly overhead. "I thought my book was really good. But maybe I was deluded. Maybe it was only fit for a bear."

"Bears ain't fussy, it's true." After dispensing this profound piece of country wisdom Vinal Pinette turned his cap around in his fingers, and Bramhall's gaze drifted toward the window. The clouds looked like bears in a chorus line, in top hats and tails, kicking up their heels.

Staring at these exuberant forms, he felt the desperate desire that had driven him all these months—to be freed from drudgery and to have a literary destiny. Longing for it twisted his guts, and then, perhaps because of his lifelong habit of depression, he let go—let go of desire, let go of his imagined destiny, let *Destiny and Desire* slip through his fingers like the string of a kite, let it fly away. He could almost see it, a golden cord whipping up into the air, out of reach. He slumped in his chair, and the golden cord went sailing, into the clouds. And he felt strangely relaxed in his ruin.

The bear entered the Port Authority building off Times Square in Manhattan. He was going back to Maine on the next Greyhound bus. The panic he'd suffered at the restaurant was only the beginning; if he attempted to stay in the human world, the buzz would cause him to crack; he'd expose himself as a bear and be put in a zoo. He carried his empty briefcase, to help him pass as a human being.

"Lemme carry that for you, sir," said a criminal in a jogging suit, to which was attached a plastic tag that said Baggage Assistant.

"No," said the bear, and cradled the empty briefcase more tightly under his arm.

"Somebody could take it from you," insisted the bogus Baggage Assistant, but the bear kept walking, past lines of down-at-the-heels travelers waiting to board buses to other places in which to be down-at-the-heels. The bear didn't know these travelers were in worse shape than he was. He didn't know they would have given anything to have an agent. He didn't know that everybody in America wanted an agent. He didn't know he was throwing away the opportunity that every true American dreams of, to be a celebrity. This was because he was a bear.

Three fun-loving skinheads who needed money saw the bear's portly, good-natured figure coming toward them and decided he'd be easy prey. They surrounded him, acting as if they knew him. "Hey, Jack, where you going with that briefcase?"

Their leader wore a Nazi helmet and had renamed himself Heimlich in honor of the man who ran the SS, not knowing he'd confused the Heimlich maneuver for rescuing choking victims and Heinrich Himmler.

"I'm not Jack," said the bear.

"Give me that briefcase," snapped Heimlich. "That's an order! *Achtung!*"

The bear stared away down the long corridor of the building, a distant look in his eyes. He didn't want to attract attention to himself, but he needn't have worried, as everyone in the Authority building was busy looking the other way.

"Give it," repeated Heimlich, pointing at the briefcase.

"Why?" asked the bear, thinking there was a problem of communication.

"We're the *Obermensch*. We take what we want." Heimlich liked to sprinkle German words into what he said. One of these days he'd take a Living Fucking Language course and astonish everyone with his German. "Now give me your wallet and that briefcase."

"No," said the stubborn bear.

The skinheads grabbed the bear by the arms, and Heimlich reached for the briefcase. The bear, feeling his only link to humanity being taken from him, gave a backhanded swipe that dislocated Heimlich's jaw and removed a sizable portion of his nose. Then he twirled Heimlich upside down, grabbed his ankles, and swung him. Heimlich's helmeted head became a blurred streak of steel striking each of the other skinheads in the face with a *whong-whong-whong* sound. Heimlich's head rattled inside the helmet, soundly concussing itself. From this point forward he would hear his treasured recording of "Deutschland über Alles" through a nice case of tinnitus.

The other skinheads had their arms up, trying to shield themselves from the blur of metal. Its impact twisted them around, breaking ribs and elbows, and a large automatic weapon bounced along the floor of the bus station. An elderly woman picked it up.

As Heimlich desperately tried to fit his nose back on, the bear looked anxiously about, afraid the crowd would attack him for such a bestial act. He started to hurry away, but now that the danger was past, the crowd applauded, crying, "Way to go" and "Nice piece of work."

And, with the automatic in her shopping bag, the elderly woman got on a bus to visit her aggravating son-in-law in New Jersey.

Arthur Bramhall followed Vinal Pinette into the entranceway of a small farmhouse. Wood was stacked neatly in the yard, and a pail of fresh water was beside the door. "What you need," said Pinette, "is more sociability. Fred'll cheer you up." He knocked on the door. "Fred, you there?"

"Come on in," said a voice from inside.

Pinette and Bramhall entered. A burly man in work pants and shirt sat by the stove. "Art," said Pinette, "this is Fred Severance. Fred, this is Art Bramhall, from up the college. I thought you and me could cheer him up."

Bramhall saw that his host was depressed, could feel it, could almost smell it.

"She left me, Vinal." Severance shook his head sadly, then remembered his duties as host. "You boys want some tea?"

The wood stove held pots and pans dented and blackened by a lifetime's use. Severance's face was reflected in the gleaming chrome of the stove, his head elongated in the metal, as if a zucchini squash were growing in his brain. Well-used harnesses hung on the wall, along with antique snowshoes. The only contemporary note was a framed color photograph of a young woman.

"That's her," said Severance, noting the direction of Bramhall's gaze. His voice was low, solemn. "World Federation of Wrastlers come to town for their annual show, and off she went."

"Cleola went off with a wrastler, did she?" inquired Pinette.

"Yes, she did. And I blame myself."

"You can't blame yourself," said Pinette.

Severance's gaze returned to the photo of his beloved. It was a studio photograph, of the kind taken at high school graduation. "I shouldn't of let her go, Vinal. Not to wrestling. 'Cause now she's out on the road with a tattooed midget."

"Her family was always fond of travel," admitted Pinette. Then, delicately, he changed the subject. "Show Art that contraption under the stove."

Severance rolled out a crudely carved length of wood, whose center was about the size and shape of a pair of bowling balls. "Beavers did that. And rolled it for miles."

Bramhall stared at the astonishing sculpture, whose mechanical utility could not be denied. It had the presence of a totem; it riveted his gaze, as if he'd met it somewhere before—his dreams of the last few nights had been terribly strange and colorful, involving all sorts of animals both real and monstrous.

Beavers, he thought to himself, they chiseled this with their teeth. But he felt how much more there was to the object than simply the tools with which the little sculptors had created it. There was an emanation coming from it, of soulful gnawing in the moonlight, while the forest was still and men were asleep. Then the beavers worked, and Bramhall, with a strange floating sensation, felt himself go to them, felt himself crouching beside them on the wooded hill above their pond, the hill down which they would roll their prize. Their eyes flashed at him, signaling a pact he could seal with them, if he desired.

With a jolt of fear, he felt himself snap back from the vision. His body twitched in the chair, as if he'd just rebounded from a long elastic swing through the forest.

"Not too many people know beavers invented the wheel," said Pinette to Bramhall. "And *that's* the kind of story—" He slapped his knee for emphasis. "—you want to tell when you get to writing your new book."

The bear pushed his shopping cart through the supermarket. The sky-scrapers of Manhattan had astounded him, and now the endless amounts of honey that man had available to him had humbled him to the ground. The intelligence, the inventiveness, the time and courage it took to lay in this much honey was the final proof that man wore the crown of creation. "Bears are just along for the ride," he said to himself as he filled his cart with honey—honey in jars, honey in plastic bottles, honey in plastic tubs.

A rainbow of colors dazzled him, and he peered more closely at the bright glass jars. Can this be? he asked himself. Excitedly, he selected an assortment of jams and jellies. When I think of the hours it would take me to pick this many blueberries . . . And there was no competition from crows, no foxes to chase away. He ignored the quiet voice within him that said that this superabundance came with a price other than the one fixed to the lid of the jars. By the time he reached the check-out counter, he had every jam jar in the store. Mounded above them were packages of cookies, cakes, pies, and doughnuts, and his respect for humanity's accomplishments was boundless.

The supermarket had narrow aisles and stock crammed everywhere. The checkout lines were long and customers smoldered with impatience. But the bear didn't mind, as it would have taken him months to gather in the forest what he'd just gathered here in a single hour. He pushed his cart in behind an elderly female. She's old, she's wise, I'll copy her. Be a golden opportunity.

"This goddamn fucking place," said the elderly female.

The bear nodded and made a mental note.

The old woman pointed a gnarled finger toward the girl working behind the checkout counter. "She's half-asleep. She don't care. We can wait here all day for the little slut." The old woman rammed her cart against the end of the checkout counter, rattling the magazine stand. "Come on, speed it up!"

The checkout woman gave the old lady a flickering glance of contempt and continued with her slow and dreamlike tallying of merchandise. The bear found her performance mesmerizing, the way she'd take hold of something, slide it along, make a bell ring, then slide it further along, to where another young woman bagged it. The movements of both women were so smooth, their manner so poised, like a particularly graceful shorebird whose antics he appreciated in salmon fishing season. The thought of this bird took him suddenly backward, to memories of his territory. Who was commanding it now? What incursions would be made into his favorite fishing spots? What other bear was even now sniffing its way into those fields he'd staked as his own? A stab of jealousy ran through him, for the unfettered step of that rival whom he could sense across hundreds of miles, a rival alone at the edge of that special field, sniffing, sniffing. Used to be one big tough sonofabitch controlled this patch. Gone. Must be dead. So then it's mine.

"Get with the program, girlie," growled the old lady, banging her cart against the counter again.

The bear angled his own cart so that he was able to bang it against the counter too, like a real human being, and in doing this he silenced the battling voices inside him.

The old lady turned toward him with a conspiratorial glance. "We oughta set fire to the place, that'd get them moving. They've only checked one goddamn item in the last minute and a half." The old lady pointed to a watch that was pinned to her coat along with a card bearing her name and address. "Don't think I haven't timed them."

The bear continued banging his cart back and forth against the checkout counter. I'm a model of deportment here.

The checkout woman totaled the old lady's order. "That'll be twenty dollars and fifty-two cents."

"Up your ass," replied the old lady. She paid, was handed her parcels, and left the store, muttering to herself.

The bear emptied his cart onto the conveyor belt. When his items had been packaged and handed to him by the bagger, he said, "Up your ass," and walked toward the door. He was learning more every day.

"What you want," said Pinette, "is a story that will touch people in the heart." They climbed into Pinette's truck and he steered them through the twilight, along the dirt road that connected the houses in the remote settlement. "I hate to see a man's suitcase stolen by a bear," continued Pinette. "Nor a child neither."

"A child?"

"Mavis Puffer, one time, was out covering her garden against the frost. She looks up and sees a figure by the fence, which could only be her old man coming home. It's dark, and Mavis never had sharp eyes. She hands her baby over the fence, says, 'Take him inside, he's cold.' Only it wasn't her old man, it was a bear." Pinette took off his cap and scratched his head, the story apparently concluded.

"And what happened to the child?"

"Bear et it, likely."

They rode in silence for several miles, Bramhall returning his gaze to the forest. He saw the glimmer of a pond through the trees, saw burnished twilight on the hillside above it, and a longing filled him, to be there, to see the beavers roll their wheel, but more important, to have them look at him, their eyes glinting, signaling.

"I believe your story is up ahead, at Armand LeBlond's place," said Pinette, and pulled his truck into the LeBlond driveway. The door to the farmhouse opened and a woman stepped out. "Armand's mother-in-law, Ada Sleeper," said Pinette meaningfully as he and Bramhall climbed from the truck, Bramhall mindful of a nearby fence, which was humming with electricity.

"How you keeping, Ada?" asked Pinette.

"Just fine, Vinal." Following this reply, a strange sound emanated from Ada Sleeper's throat, like the cackling of a hen. And then her voice became normal again. "Armand's in the south meadow. He'll be back soon."

"And Janetta?"

"In the barn," said Ada, the hen-cackle sounding in her throat once more. "Janetta!"

A young woman came out from the barn. Behind her Bramhall saw lighted stalls and the forms of cows.

"Company, Janetta," announced Ada with cackle.

Janetta LeBlond came across the yard, smiling tentatively at the two men. Introductions were made, and Pinette engaged her in conversation, during which he several times sent knowing nods toward Bramhall, whose significance Bramhall failed to understand. Then Armand

41

LeBlond came across the field, and Pinette and Bramhall went to meet him. "How're you, mah friend?" asked LeBlond in a buoyant Maine-French accent.

"I brung this feller to see you, Armand. He's a writer looking for a story."

LeBlond drew out a pouch of tobacco and paper and rolled himself a cigarette whose ragged ends ignited in a sputtering rush of flame. He glanced at Bramhall. "You talk to Mudder-in-Law, you hear how she sound like chicken?"

"I did notice, yes," said Bramhall.

"Well, Janetta used to sound like chicken too. It run in dat family." LeBlond puffed on his homemade cigarette thoughtfully. "Very queer damn business. But den one night, Janetta had too much to drink and she c'lapse into mah fence." He pointed to it, and the fence seemed to hum slightly louder, making a chord, as if proud of the part it had played.

"She musta spent too much time hanging there," explained Pinette, "because it took the cackle right out of 'er."

"Den de old woman want to t'row herself against dat fence too, get rid of cackle same way. But I tell her, dere's no one like you wid chickens, Mudder-in-Law." As LeBlond said this, Bramhall noticed that several chickens were devotedly following Ada, clucking up against her ankles. LeBlond turned to Bramhall. "I give you dozen eggs, you tell me. Best damn eggs you ever eat, I bet."

The three men stood quietly then, as the last light of the day was lost over the fields. Later, in the truck, with a bowl of eggs on the seat between himself and Bramhall, Pinette said, "A remarkable true story, Art, which I believe has all the trimmings."

Bramhall picked up one of the eggs and cradled it softly in his palm. Then he put its cool surface against his slightly fevered forehead. It had a soothing effect.

"Porkapine going," said Pinette, nodding ahead of them, where the ambling creature was caught in the headlights of the slowing vehicle. Its eyes gleamed, and Bramhall got out of the truck while it was still moving. He followed the porcupine across the road, which caused it to raise its quills defensively. It waddled off into the foliage, and he listened to it going slowly away into the darkness of its own concerns.

"Porkapines are comical rigs, all right," said Pinette, coming up beside him in the road.

Bramhall was sniffing the porcupine, its odor somewhat human, like a heavily perspiring person in a raunchy undershirt.

"What's up, Art? You smell something?"

"You don't smell it?"

"Can't say I do."

The porcupine had gone far enough into the underbrush for the sound of its movements to go undetected, but its odor was leaving a vivid picture of it in the night air. Bramhall turned his head around, suddenly aware that he was smelling a night rich with scents of every kind. But the moment he tried to analyze the sensation, something slammed shut, with the sound of a filing cabinet, a door, a window whose sash has snapped, and that snap was his return from whatever perfumed cloud he'd been traveling on, and his heightened sense of smell was gone.

Elliot Gadson was reading the final proofs of an autobiography written by acquitted society scion Barton Balfour III, who'd been accused of having disposed of his wife by serving her up to guests in a light Madeira mushroom sauce. Balfour's prose style left much to be desired, but the main thing was that the *heart* was there.

"Mr. Hal Jam to see you, Mr. Gadson." A young editorial assistant stood at the door, the bear beside her.

"Ah, Hal, come in, come in. I'm delighted to meet you." Gadson came around to the front of his desk, holding out his hand. "I loved your book. It was completely real to me. I felt I'd known the people in it all my life."

The bear was sniffing the office: coffee, cologne, paper, glue. He liked the life-size cardboard replica of Barton Balfour III with a knife and fork in his hands; it showed a proper esteem for eating.

"I can't remember the last time I read such an absorbing work," continued Gadson, feeling his way carefully, as Jam had the air of a messenger boy who'd been sniffing aerosol cans. "Noticing our other titles? As you can see, we have a diversified list. A star biography or two, the latest from the Bel Air Diet Doctor . . ."

Gadson was not warming to his new author, for Jam was guarded. God, I hope he's not homophobic, thought Gadson, whose wall carried a poster of Cary Grant in *Bringing Up Baby*, at the moment when he'd put on a woman's nightgown and cried, *"I just went gay all of a sudden."*

The bear was not homophobic, as bears have a tolerant sexual attitude. Occasionally young male bears who fail to find a female will hump each other, and no one makes a fuss about it.

"I'd like you to meet Bettina Quint, our publicity director," said Gadson, and dialed another office. "Hal Jam is with me now, Bettina."

The bear had turned to look out the window, over the bustling city. "Mine," he said, making his territorial claim. Of course, to firm it up he'd have to shit along the perimeter. All in good time. Hearing a sound at the door, he turned back around, and had the impression that a confused hummingbird had just entered the room.

Bettina Quint was tiny and moved with great speed. A rapid shift of trajectory, upon spying Hal Jam, caused her to strike a stack of books and send them flying. "Oh shit," she said, and started picking them up.

"Please, leave them," said Gadson with a patient air.

"This is my second collision of the afternoon. The

first one was much more colorful." Bettina attempted to adjust her flyaway bun of streaked-blond hair. An emerald scarf encircled her twenty-two-inch waist; her constant hurrying flight burned calories in a steady flame. She rushed to her new writer and shot out her hand. "Your book is going to be a blockbuster."

Bettina spoke as a hummingbird might, in high-pitched peeps of great excitement. The bear sniffed her discreetly, taking in the aroma of her perfume, makeup, deodorant, hand and face cream, and the faint residue of the soap she'd showered with. Her resemblance to a hummingbird pleased him, for hummingbirds were close to bees in their habits.

Bettina had already made her own assessment of the new young writer the Muses had sent off the assembly line. From her reading of a three-paragraph synopsis of Jam's book she'd concluded that he was the find of the year—a writer who could move a woman to tears of compassion for herself. She regretted not having had time to read the book—it seemed like fun—but that was a luxury she couldn't afford just yet. The interviewers she'd be wooing wouldn't have time to read the book either; they'd be working from her publicity release. Something so drab as the book itself wasn't much use to anyone.

"I'm like the Shadow, Hal. I cloud men's minds. I've got a big budget for *Destiny and Desire*, and that means I'm going to impose you on the national consciousness." Bettina moved as she spoke, sitting, standing, sitting again, this time on a papier-mâché fishing frog from Java which Gadson kept at the edge of his desk. "I'm not talking a brief moment of exposure here and there, I'm talking major saturation. I'm sorry, Elliot, was this a precious memento?"

"Ignore it, darling."

"To saturate we have to tour long and hard, Hal. We have to give the public a feeling of intimacy with you." Bettina paced to the window and back, then to Gadson's couch, ideas seeming to propel her as they surfaced. Her hands were continually gesturing, and the bear watched her dizzily, his nose working back and forth. She smells sincere, he said to himself.

"We'll make the Hemingway comparison, I hope you don't mind. Sportsman, adventurer, larger than life, the man of action who can also tell a love story. You have a wonderful physical presence, I can feel it with you just standing there, can't you, Elliot, a sort of raw vitality? Forgive me, Hal, I have to treat my authors as objects. You have charisma, and I want to capitalize on it. We'll play up your love of the outdoors but I'd like to put an environmental slant on it, the sacredness of nature, how you respect it. If you've shot any endangered species play that down—in fact I wouldn't mention it at all. *I* don't mind if you killed any cute little animals, but some people might."

"I kill when I have to."

"Certainly, perfect, kill when you have to." Bettina spun toward Gadson, as if he were a waiting flower, and shot toward him. "Hal's voice is amazing. When audio rights are sold, he should be the one reading it, he's perfect." She darted back toward the bear, her high-pitched voice chirping on about all that she had in mind for him. The bear rose from his chair and stepped over to the door frame, where he vigorously rubbed his back against it. A suggestible brute, he was seeing fields of flowers again, with hummingbirds darting over them. He went down on the floor and rolled around on his back.

Gadson was on the phone immediately to Boykins. "Your client is in my office, rolling on the floor." Gadson looked at Bettina. "Chum says he does this kind of thing, but that it passes."

Bettina stared at the bear in horrified fascination. His feet were pedaling at the air as he manipulated his spine, twisting first one way and then the other, with a vaguely obscene look in his eyes. Would *Good Morning America* appreciate a guest who might go down on all fours? She looked at Gadson. "Can we tour with this?"

"Not to Dalton's in the mall, we can't."

Bettina looked back at the deliriously squirming novelist. "What if we called it performance art?"

"Performance epilepsy is more like it," said Gadson.

Bettina's gaze remained fixed on Hal Jam. Uncontrollable velocity sometimes sent her tumbling to the floor herself, and though her recovery was always swift it was nonetheless embarrassing. The interesting thing about Hal Jam was that he was making it pay off for him. Far from looking embarrassed, he seemed incredibly self-confident and vital. "I can work with it," she said decisively.

"His book is so solemn," said Gadson. "It's hard to square it with what I'm looking at now. I don't say I mind him rolling around on the floor, but I do think it'll be hard for you to package it."

The bear was about scratched out, however. The faces of the two people in the room came back into focus and he realized his perspective could only be that of one who was on the floor making a spectacle of himself again. A sheepish grin crossed his face, and he sat upright.

"Feeling better?" asked Gadson with concern.

The bear was looking at Bettina. Little birds had always seemed so intelligent to him, their dainty ways of food gathering so different from his own rough methods; and this hummingbird woman was so intensely focused, her eyes glittered with such interest in him—he sensed she was to be his teacher. He stretched out a paw toward her.

"Yes, dear, I'm here." Bettina was used to needy writers.

"I confess I'm touched," said Gadson. It was obvious that Jam's gruff exterior hid a sensitive nature, vulnerable as a child's. He whispered to Bettina, "A touch of autism, valiantly overcome? Is there an angle there for you?"

Bettina gazed at Jam thoughtfully as he climbed up off the floor, his ungainly form seeming to balance itself with difficulty. Yet once his feet were set, he exuded that same tremendous presence. "Christ, what a combination. Strong but wounded. Women are going to love him. I'll need to know a lot about your life, Hal. Because somewhere in all of it are the charming little bits that make great publicity."

"Well, good-bye," said the bear, who could only take so much human company at a time. Central Park was calling to him; he needed the gnarly emanations of trees to settle his mind, which the city greatly agitated. He turned toward the door, and Bettina rocketed off after him. Her sleeve caught on the outstretched cardboard arm of Barton Balfour III, and the display dummy toppled over, his hand running down her back and catching in the bright scarf that circled her tiny waist. "Oh god, he's following me. Elliot!"

"Coming, darling," said Gadson, and he disentangled Bettina from Balfour's arm.

"Did I ruin him?"

"He's resilient. You'd better hurry if you're going to catch Jam."

"I like him, don't you?"

"With certain reservations."

"Well, at least he hasn't served anyone in mushroom sauce." Bettina made another quick attempt to straighten her flyaway hair and raced off down the hall; editors in their cubicles had the sense of a brightly colored projectile sailing by. Cavendish Press was owned by Tempo Oil, and when Bettina shot into the elevator after the bear, it was into the company of conservative Texas oilmen. They knew that Bettina was quite high up at Cavendish, but they couldn't imagine how she'd ever got to that position careening through the building as she did, like a prairie dog shitting chili peppers.

As she and the bear stepped out onto Madison Avenue, a taxi pulled in beside them at the curb and Boykins leapt out. "I came as soon as I could. Hal, are you all right?"

"Let's eat," said the bear, pointing at a hot dog vendor's cart.

"He seems all right," said Boykins to Bettina. "Was it a severe attack?"

"I'd say moderate." Bettina and Boykins were a striking pair, gesturing simultaneously with the fine frenzy of a windmill farm.

"Hal, do you know what causes these seizures?" asked Boykins.

"Hot dogs," said the bear, holding up one in each paw.

"I suppose I shouldn't ask," said Boykins. "After all,

it's none of my business." Boykins was repeatedly running his finger out into the air and back to the tip of his nose. Since taking Jam as a client, his obsessions had started to increase, after years of moderate hibernation. He looked at Bettina nervously. "Where are you two going?"

"We're just getting to know each other. Why don't you walk with us, Chum?" Bettina was studying Jam from the corner of her eye. He was as quiet as a plate of toast. Would he be able to provide the media with snappy sound bites?

"We got a Book-of-the-Month Club sale, Bettina, did you know?" asked Boykins.

"I heard, congratulations."

The bear strode along, his equilibrium restored. There was food everywhere. Mine, he said to himself, all mine.

They passed a toy store with a huge Mickey Mouse in the window, and Boykins had a terrible memory of himself at age twelve in Disneyland, immobilized because he'd had to genuflect every time he saw Mickey Mouse.

"Park," said the bear, turning west toward the scent of brackish water.

A balloon vendor stood at the edge of the park, large inflated animals floating on strings above his head, among them—Mickey Mouse.

Kneel, said Mickey to Boykins. *Or terrible misfortune will befall your client.*

"Did I drop something . . ." Boykins went down on one knee in front of the imperious balloon.

"Come on, Chum, he's getting ahead of us." Bettina grabbed Boykins by the elbow and hauled him upright. Boykins turned his head back toward the floating mouse. "I was thinking . . . of . . . of buying it for my children."

"I didn't know you had children."

"I have one . . . a distant one . . ."

"A distant child?"

"Cousin."

"Chum, are you all right?"

"No, I'm not. I'm having an attack of obsessive-compulsive disorder. I'm going to wind up in a straitjacket, Bettina."

"Are you worried about having left the stove on, something like that?"

"I'm worried about Hal."

They were descending the path into the park. The bear was already below them, beside the lake.

"He's erratic," said Boykins, "and I keep wanting to control him."

"I'm a good judge of character about three days a week," said Bettina, "so don't take my view of the matter. But—" She pointed toward Jam, who was staring into the lake. "—this isn't someone you can control."

"He's a gold mine, Bettina. He's the jelly on the

bagel of my life. What if he has an attack in traffic?" They reached the bottom of the sloping path and walked toward their author.

At the edge of the pond a child in a sailor suit was operating a radio-controlled submarine. His English nanny was seated on a nearby park bench reading a tabloid whose cover story was Princess Di's new romance, with a handsome space alien, who beamed her up out of London each night and gave her the tender sex she so deserved.

The bear was staring at a faint turbulence on the pond. His eyes narrowed into slits as the turbulence came nearer. He saw a smooth, elongated shape glistening beneath the water; his tongue raced over his snout. He jumped into the pond and swiftly struck.

"Hal!" Boykins and Bettina reached him just as the bear's jaws closed on the submarine. There was a sound of crunching plastic. Springs and computer chips appeared in the bear's teeth.

"Nanny, Nanny, he ate my submarine!"

Tough, thought the bear, munching on what he assumed were the fish's skull and bones. Very little flavor at all. Must be old.

Bettina tried to pull her new writer out of the water. He pivoted away from her, she held on, and found herself dangling in the air. A moment later she was standing in the muck of the pond. "Oh god, these are my three-hundred-dollar French rip-off shoes. I just know they're going to dissolve . . ."

"Nanny, Nanny!"

The bear spit out more pieces of the fish. The submarine's rudder and conning tower sank into the pond as he shook his head in disgust. Not a tasty bit of flesh on that catch, he remarked to himself.

"Nanny, it's ruined!"

Nanny put down her paper reluctantly and walked over to the bear. The bear looked at Nanny, then at Bettina and Boykins. He looked down at his feet and saw his new shoes were full of water and his pants were wet up to the knees. Am I making a bad impression here? he wondered, removing the last bits from his mouth. "Fish," he said by way of explanation.

"Bettina," said Boykins, helping her out of the pond, "are you all right? I'm so sorry."

"Not your fault, Chum. Publicists are used to wading in shit."

The sailor-suited little boy angrily threw his radio control into the pond.

"I'll pay for it," said Boykins. "How much?"

"A thousand dollars," said the child, whose father was a bond trader.

Boykins held out two fifties. Nanny took the money

quickly and slipped it in her purse. Profitable incidents like this came a nanny's way all too rarely.

Boykins, pretending to look into the pond, genuflected.

"All bones," said the bear, thinking his agent was trying to spy out a fish for himself.

Boykins rose to his feet and stared at his client. Jam seemed indifferent to having just eaten a child's toy. The child was being led away in tears and Jam was calmly picking his teeth. He knows something about life I don't know, said Boykins to himself, and I'm going to learn it.

Bettina fell into step on the other side of Jam, her three-hundred-dollar French shoes squishing water. Apart from that, her get-acquainted period with her new author was no worse than usual. A public figure who destroyed children's toys *could* be an interesting publicity sell, with the right angle. "Did you do it because you think children have been exploited by the toy industry?"

"Bad fishing," said the bear. He was, as Bettina'd hoped, an environmentalist.

Bettina reflected on his reply. *Hal Jam, renowned sportsman, sums up society's problem this way: Bad fishing.*

A sound bite with potential.

"She's all that's left of the old Spooner place," said Vinal Pinette, laying his hand against a dilapidated henhouse. "Titus Spooner was the greatest hand for inventing stuff I ever saw. The problem was he invented things which had no earthly use. Put your shoulder against it with me—"

Bramhall pushed with Pinette. "Harder," said Pinette, "she's froze up."

Bramhall was adrift in Pinette's literary suggestions, wherever they might take him. Lately they all seemed connected to hens. He pushed harder, felt the henhouse give, and a creaking sound came from somewhere below its floor.

"That's it," said Pinette. "Get your back into it."

They strained and the structure began to slowly rotate, bending the grass beneath it. They turned it several degrees against the horizon before stopping, out of breath. "It used to be you could turn it with one finger," said Pinette.

"But why would anyone want to turn it?"

"For rotating hens in their nests. Titus felt a hen should face each direction once a day." Pinette peered through the broken window of the henhouse. "The mechanics were first-rate, but the basic idea was weak because it don't matter which jeezly way a hen faces. Everything Titus come up with had that sort of flaw in 'er. Titus's old woman used to give him hell about wasting time on inventions, said it were going to ruin them." Pinette brought his head back out of the window. "And now the whole damn shooting match has rotated off the face of the earth, Titus and his old woman included."

Pinette peered at his friend, trying to see if he was getting his point across. "Don't that sound like a better book than the one you lost? We'll write it up together, you and me, and put the son-of-a-whore in a cast-iron safe." Pinette pushed against the henhouse again, and this time it gave more easily, moving several degrees on its rusted track. "I don't say Titus's rotating chicken house were the Seventh Wonder of the World, but the look in them hens' eyes when they started spinning was notable."

Bramhall stood in silence with Pinette then, paying his respects to the vanished inventor's dream.

A weasel stuck its head up from beneath a corner of the building.

"He'd eat us if he could," said Pinette. "Fears nawthing on god's earth, if he can get a neck bite."

The weasel examined Bramhall with what seemed to be disdain for one so clumsy, so slow, so hopelessly out of touch with the currents that shape a weasel to its purpose.

"Comes from a long line of chicken killers," said Pinette as the weasel vanished.

Bramhall felt a lethal swiftness still quivering in the air, a sort of disturbance the weasel had left behind. Bramhall turned abruptly, sensing the direction of the invisible ripple as his gaze tracked over the high grass. Precisely where his gaze stopped, the weasel reappeared. The animal rose up on his back legs, and Bramhall could feel the little killer reassessing him, perhaps more favorably.

"It's so fortunate I happened to be in New York just now," said Zou Zou Sharr to the bear over cocktails at Elaine's bar. Before becoming an agent for the Creative Management Corporation, she'd directed the Bel Air Diet Doctor's empire and maintained her slender shape with his naturally artificially flavored products. She had a fiery-red crown of power hair and a meltingly compassionate smile, which, when she was challenged by anyone, congealed to ice, as did her bright blue eyes. "It's so much nicer to deal with an author in person," she said to Jam. "I'm wild about the book, of course," she added, having read the coverage on it written by her agency's eighteen-year-old reader.

The bear looked at Zou Zou Sharr from under the peak of his baseball cap. It was the first time he'd been this close to a human female for any length of time, and he liked the experience. If she had some fur on her face and the backs of her hands she might be good-looking.

"We've already handled some of the biggest books of the season," continued Zou Zou, "and I know we'll be able to run with yours."

Zou Zou was genuinely enthusiastic despite not having read the book. In showbiz, books were always a question mark, because books were just books, but buzz you could trust. Zou Zou understood buzz, was a connoisseur of buzz, and went from buzz to buzz like a flower looking for bees. And the buzz on Hal Jam's book was big.

The bear adjusted his tail with a surreptitious move of the paw, getting himself more comfortable in the restaurant chair. He was in the mood for some soda pop. Fizz on the lips, little tingly bubbles up the nose, that was life in the fast lane for a bear. Why should he have any regrets? A bear lives in the moment. He ignores the tiny voice, like that of a flower, that whispers inside him, *There's a stream below the wooded hill, there are fish in the pools, come back, come back.*

"I've talked to your editor and your publicist," said Zou Zou. "Your campaign is going to be tremendous." Zou Zou leaned back in her chair and let her gaze wander momentarily around the tables at Elaine's; she was glad to be out of L.A. She'd recently broken off a relationship with a young director who liked to make love while watching uncut footage of *The Battleship Potemkin*. Now whenever she thought of becoming intimate with a man her mind filled with the image of a baby carriage bouncing down a flight of stairs. She leaned closer to the bear and fixed him with her compassionate blue gaze. "You've got a great team going for you, and CMC wants to be part of it.

My associates are standing by their telephones right now, waiting to hear that you're going to sign with us." In fact, she'd been remiss in not getting to Jam earlier, but she'd been too destroyed by the battleship *Potemkin* to focus on the buzz.

Her perfume was curling past the bear's nostrils, a light, delicate scent. He gave himself a strong reminder that he must not express his emotions by rolling around on the floor, although it'd be a good way to look for more briefcases. Chum Boykins had told him that a lot of writers went to Elaine's, and a lot of writers meant a lot of briefcases.

"What I love about your book," continued Zou Zou, "is that it's so believable, and yet politically correct. I adore how unashamedly you bring in the issue of women's rights."

"You smell good."

Zou Zou Sharr smiled uncertainly. Generally, she'd have thrown a sexist comment like that back in the face of the man who made it, but she'd just got done complimenting Jam for his position on women's rights. Also, since he hadn't yet signed the agreement with Creative Management—which was her fault entirely—she decided to be old-fashioned about the insult, and let her smile spread to its dazzlingly fullest. But even while turning up the wattage of her eyes, lips, and teeth, she wasn't perfectly at ease with Hal Jam. He didn't talk money or percentages and when a potential client didn't talk money or percentages it could mean they'd already written her and her agency off. Which was a nightmare she couldn't allow to happen because she'd have to face the totally justified anger of Creative Management. They might even fire her, because she'd been sensing that she was a threat to certain fragile male egos there. Zou Zou's ego was fragile too, but it was contained in indestructible packaging, like a Bel Air Diet Cookie, whose shelf life was 750 years. "I want you to feel free to call upon me anytime, Hal, night or day. I'm sure you'll have lots of questions about the way things work in Hollywood, and you should get straight answers. I'll have them for you. You'll always get the truth from me."

The waiter laid a basket of bread and buns on the table, and a dish of butter patties. The waiter's clothing was saturated with the smells of the kitchen, and the bear fought down the urge to butter the waiter's arm and eat it. Moments like these are the hardest, he reflected to himself. He made himself reach politely for a bun, and buttered it slowly. His method was to completely cover a bun with butter patties, all of them.

Zou Zou watched, transfixed. She hadn't eaten butter in a decade.

The bear swallowed the bun. A dab of butter remained fixed to his nose. His long red tongue came out, nabbed the morsel, and swirled it inward.

"I see that you enjoy eating," said Zou Zou nervously. Over the years, she'd had a recurrent dream of floating in an ocean of warm butter, on a buoyant bun. If she ate the bun, she'd drown in her own cellulite.

"More," said the bear to the waiter, pointing at the empty butter dish.

Zou Zou turned her wineglass slowly in her long, delicate fingers and tried not to think of the number of calories that'd just been devoured in front of her. "When you think of Destiny and Desire as a movie, who do you see in the leading role?"

"Popcorn," said the bear. He'd followed its haunting scent one day, and in this way discovered movies. The movies had meant little, but the hot buttered popcorn had been a revelation.

There's something going on here, thought Zou Zou to herself. Hal Jam is playing the country bumpkin role to put me off my stride. I know he's not a bumpkin, because bumpkins don't get big buzz. Bumpkins don't get to talk to women like me.

"You're saying you don't care who plays the lead. You're indifferent. I understand, of course. You're an artist, you live in god's country. What we do in Hollywood doesn't matter to you, and after all, why should it?" Zou Zou leaned closer and spoke more intimately, the way she used to speak to people who didn't know they needed a diet shake composed entirely of edible foamy plastic, who didn't know how truly nutritious plastic was. "But perhaps it does matter, Hal. Creative Management can deliver big stars, and big stars mean bigger profits at the back end."

"Popcorn and butter," said the bear.

"I admit it, back-end money is just puff with a little grease on it, I admit there's no real substance there. But no other agency can guarantee back-end money for you either." She stared deeply into his dark eyes. His expression of innocence was deceptive. Obviously he knew how the negotiation game was played, was hinting he had an alternative. She shifted gears. "You're from Maine," she said. "It must be paradise to live there."

"Not enough honey."

Zou Zou frowned. He wasn't going to be diverted. "Hal, I promise that we'll get you the sweetest deal in the business. We're dedicated to getting bonuses for our clients all along the line, beginning from the first day of production."

"Ice cream every day," said the bear. If they were talking about contracts, he wanted to nail the important points.

She shook her head sadly. "I can't get you a bonus for every day of shooting. I wish I could. But nobody can get you that."

"With nuts sprinkled on."

She could see he was going to be unreasonable.

"And lots of whipped cream." He banged his paw on

the table. He knew how these things should be served, and he wouldn't take it without nuts and whipped cream.

"Well," she sighed, "we do have one actress—I don't want to mention names—but we got it into her contract that every day when she appears on the set there's a fabulous gift spontaneously waiting for her. Some days it's a fabulous bracelet, some days it's a fabulous watch, whatever. We'll see if we can get you a fabulous gift for every day of shooting, fabulous to be defined by our lawyers, not the studio's. How's that?"

"With a cherry on top."

God, thought Zou Zou, with men it always comes down to sex. She crossed her legs, her skirt riding up to midthigh; then she turned toward him in her chair, though she'd *never* use sex to make a sale. "I hear the sailing in Maine is wonderful. Do you sail?"

"I fish."

"Well, of course your book is filled with it." She leaned toward him, wanting him to know that in spite of her business orientation, she was sensitive to literature. "I suppose you can tell—I'm passionate about your work."

The bear looked down at her legs. It was too bad she shaved them. He glanced back up at her. "Let it grow," he said.

Not dreaming that a man could be telling her to let the hair on her legs grow, Zou Zou placed his remark in the general texture of their conversation. "Letting it grow *is* the organic approach to the artist/agent relationship, of course, but we can't let that relationship grow too *slowly*, Hal. We do need a signed agreement." She reached across the table and touched his arm. "As I said, I'm *passionate* about the project." Zou Zou intended to spend her old age in the South of France with two young weight lifters to carry her around. A comfortable retirement required that she make big money *now*, and so she allowed her hand to remain on Jam's wrist.

Her nails were long and red, a cosmetic touch the bear found hard to adjust to. He growled, and she drew her hand back, her blue eyes focusing like particle-beam weapons. "All right, Hal. Why don't you just level with me? What else is it about the agreement you're not happy with?"

The bear sipped his wine and tried to contribute something meaningful to the conversation. "I hear you like pie."

"You think Creative Management's cut of the pie is too big? Any agency that takes less than we do doesn't have the clout. They'll promise you a lot, but they won't deliver. We have the directors, and we have the stars. Believe me, Hal, your piece of the pie is just what it should be, and so is CMC's."

"When I eat a pie, I eat it all."

"Of course you do, and I understand. The book is

yours, it's your creation, and you want your fair share." Zou Zou was sweating now as she realized that he *must* be talking to other agencies. "I know what you're unhappy about. It's the percentage we take, isn't it? Well, we'll cut it from fifteen to fourteen and a half. Do you know why? Because your book reached me on a visceral level, and I must have it. I know I'm destined to be the one representing it." She put a hand to her chest, spreading her fingers dramatically.

The bear stared back at her, bearish thoughts moving in his head, of loping along a country road at sunset. The old territory was signaling him. Would he ever see it again? Zou Zou took his mournful stare to mean *no sale*. She felt the floor of Elaine's turning into edible plastic foam, and she saw herself doggie paddling in diet shakes again.

The Creative Management suite in the Plaza hotel is furnished like a little piece of Hollywood away from home. The bear stood in this den of opulence, deeply embarrassed, because a female stood across from him, waiting for him to perform the mating act, and he couldn't.

Zou Zou, standing in her underwear, was equally embarrassed. She'd panicked about losing him as a client and had started coming out of her clothes. He'd gone along with it, had seemed to encourage it, but now his eyes were darting around nervously, and clearly he wanted to leave. God, she thought to herself, he's impotent, and I've forced him to admit it. How could I have been so stupid? She took a step toward him, then hesitated. "I'm so sorry, Hal. I've acted like a fool."

The bear struggled to reply. People talked, that's what they did the most of. But he had so little to say, and anyway what do you say to a human female in heat? He growled under his breath. When she'd taken him to this den of hers, he thought it was for more dessert. Then she'd made some suggestive movements, but they weren't big and lumbering, with drooling and growling. She hadn't snarled and wriggled her backside suggestively. That's what turned a bear on. Human females just didn't know how to get a bear going.

"Hal, I'll tell you the truth. My job may be on the line. Money is tight and if I don't get you signed, I could be fired." Zou Zou straightened her slip strap, edged her stockinged feet into her shoes. "Please, can you forgive me?"

The bear's nostrils widened as he desperately sought for a smell that would put springtime in his heart and restore his pride. He was a sovereign of the forest. With lady bears he'd struggled valiantly and they'd surrendered as he'd subdued them with his majesty. Then he'd strolled off for something to eat, and everyone was satisfied. But now he'd failed and was mortified.

. . .

An exhausted Zou Zou stood at the window of the Plaza suite, staring down through the twilight to the lake in Central Park. Hal was asleep. She sat down beside him and ran her hand lightly along his leg. "You're an animal in bed," she said softly.

He'd been slow getting started but once he was in motion, she'd never known anything like it. He'd suddenly lifted her right off the floor and tossed her around like a doll. That, and the prospect of drowning in diet shake, had acted as a powerful aphrodisiac. And then his noises—the grunts and the bellowing, the thrillingly incomprehensible things he'd growled in her ear—just amazing. And his technique was so totally original, the way he'd spun her around and bitten her on the back of the neck and then—well, when he came it felt like someone christening the battleship *Potemkin*.

Zou Zou gazed at Hal's deceptively corpulent figure. Behind that shy, backward facade was a heroic lover. The incongruity of it all was so intriguing, that this quiet pudge was as great a lover as he was a writer. But he still hadn't signed the contract. Now, she thought, while he's mellowed out. But first, let's get some champagne into him. She took a bottle from the ice bucket and pried up against the cork.

The cork blew and the bear sprang out of bed,

knocking over the table lamp, whose bulb burst with a
noise like another rifle shot. The hunters were after him!
He thundered toward the window, ripped the drapes
down, and butted his head through the glass, his only
concern to reach the trees he saw beyond him. Zou Zou
grabbed him from behind just as a knock sounded at the
door. She shouted over her shoulder, "Come in! Help
me!"

The room service waiter entered. He was a middle-
aged Frenchman with a face of boundless guile. "How may
I be of assistance, madame?"

"How? Jesus Christ, he's trying to jump!"

"Very good, madame." The waiter ran to the window, grabbed the guest by the ankles, and gave him a good
yank backward, a maneuver he was practiced in, for rock
stars frequently stayed at the hotel.

"Don't let go!" cried Zou Zou.

The waiter dutifully held the guest's brawny legs and
said to him, "Monsieur, you have everything to live for."
He was, as he said this, looking through Madame's open
nightgown.

"Yes, Hal! You're going to be rich! You're *it!* You're
going to be a *household word!*"

The bear sniffed at the air. He was smelling the steak
he ordered. He turned slowly and saw the food-laden cart
in the doorway.

"You're in my hotel room," said Zou Zou softly. "You're safe."

The bear glanced down at the room service waiter clinging to his legs. "Am I under arrest?" He didn't ask the more terrible question, *And will I be put in a zoo?*

"Of course not, monsieur," said the waiter. "This is the Plaza." He rose, adjusting his tie.

The bear lifted the silver lid covering his steak, and Zou Zou gave the waiter a fifty. "I'm grateful for your help."

"Not at all, madame." The waiter turned with a soft, discreet step, and the door made hardly a sound as he closed it behind him.

The bear was nibbling from the food cart. His panic was forgotten now, because he was eating, and because he was a bear.

Zou Zou stood beside him. "You had a nightmare. You woke from it suddenly and were disoriented. At Creative Management we're used to working with disoriented artists. We understand the *pressures* that rise up inside a man like you. Hal—" She laid the CMC writer/agent agreement on the food cart. "—we're in your corner. Let's make it official, shall we, and put your mind at rest on that point? With CMC representing you, you'll have agents who *care* for you." She handed him the pen. "Just your signature, Hal, so you can feel more secure."

With great slowness, the bear managed to sign his name, his brow furrowed as he gazed down at the slowly forming letters that spelled his human identity. When he'd finished the signature, he looked up, not without a little pride in his accomplishment.

"I'm so happy, Hal," said Zou Zou as she saw the sea of diet shake receding from her; its billowing plastic foam would remain the business of other eager sea goddesses running the weight-loss industry, tridents prodding the too-plump backsides of humanity. She quickly folded the agreement back into her briefcase. "And now we can relax." She put her arms around his neck. His intoxicating scent was like nothing she'd ever smelled before. "I usually don't let this happen," she said, pressing her body against him.

He sensed she wanted to repeat what they'd done earlier. She couldn't know how difficult it had been for him to perform with her, how he'd had to imagine her covered with fur.

Vinal Pinette led the way toward the cookhouse of the logging operation, his dog trailing behind him, and Bramhall bringing up the rear. "The crew's out cutting," said Pinette, "but Ransome Spatt'll be here. He's the feller we want."

Bramhall heard the far-off buzzing of chain saws, and then a nearer buzzing caught his ear, of a bee sailing past him. His jaws snapped, and the bee was imprisoned in his mouth. He spit it out in horror, and the stunned bee fell onto a blade of grass, where it clung momentarily, using its legs to wipe the saliva off its wings.

Bramhall heard a splash of water and turned toward the cookhouse. A portly man in a gray sleeveless undershirt stood in the doorway, a dripping basin in his hands. "Why, Vinal Pinette! You old mushrat, how you been?"

"Still standing, Ransome."

Bramhall and Pinette followed Ransome Spatt inside. Two large wood stoves were at the center of the room, with pots steaming on both of them. Pans of fresh bread and rolls were on a rough-hewn table by the window.

"Tear into them buns," said Spatt, sliding butter and jam toward Bramhall. "It might be all you'll get today."

"Got a full crew?" asked Pinette.

"We do." Spatt stirred six spoons of sugar into his tea. "But we could use an experienced man, Vinal. Teach these young Turks what it's all about."

"I'm into the book writing business now," said Pinette.

"Didn't know you was a hand for writing."

"I'm providing the raw material," said Pinette. "Art's the writer."

Bramhall nodded cordially, but he was still trying to deal with the fact that only minutes ago he'd nailed a bee midflight with his jaws.

"But all Art can think about is bears," Pinette was saying, "so I figure that our book'll have to be about bears."

"Well, you come to the right person." Spatt broke off a bun and sliced it carefully open. "I found my little bear cub in the woods out back. He'd got separated from his mama and was crying his goddamned heart out, so's I moved him in here. He had a bunk right there behind the stove." Spatt pointed with his knife. "We arm-wrestled that little feller every night right at this here table, and there wasn't a man in the camp could beat him. Ain't that so, Vinal?"

Pinette nodded. "And that cub weren't but six months old."

"The little son-of-a-whore loved ice cream," said Spatt. "He'd sit there with a cone just like you or me and lick it all up with that big tongue of his. The 'spression on his face was something to see. Then at night when we was jawing, he'd sit where you're sitting—" Spatt directed his gaze at Bramhall. "—and listen to the men talk."

"I believe," said Pinette, "he understood every word we said."

"When you get to know a bear," said Spatt, "you see how much brains they got." He blew across the edge of his teacup. "Well, sir, one night his mama come for him." He pointed toward the back of the cookhouse. "Started digging a hole underneath the floor. There ain't nothing more dangerous than Mother Bear when she's been separated from her cub. She'd have torn the foundation right out of the place to get in, so I opened the door to let the cub run join her. But do you know, the little son-of-a-whore didn't want to go. He just stood there staring at his mama, and then he turned around and climbed back up onto his bunk, as if he had something important to do there."

"He liked ice cream that much," explained Pinette to Bramhall with a knowing nod.

"Well, Mama Bear wasn't going to stand for that

nonsense," continued Spatt. "She come right in the door and give us a look that said we'd better not mess with her."

"We didn't neither," said Pinette.

"She lifted her cub up by the scruff of the neck and the little bugger whined to beat hell, but she dragged him outa there. He and Mama Bear went trotting off in the moonlight with Mama licking him and scolding him at the same time. And he looked back over his shoulder at all of us, as if he had plans for coming back."

Pinette placed his big woodsman's hands on the edge of the table and rocked in his chair. "I've knowed a fair number of animals in my day, and not one of them was as smart as that bear cub. Now, you take this dog of mine here—" He pointed toward the beast, who looked up at him guiltily, aware by the old man's tone that one of his poorer performances was coming under discussion. "He broke into the feed room and ate a fifty-pound bag of chow in one sitting. Swelled up like a bullfrog, and was so stuffed he couldn't even move his tail. Sorriest-looking rig you ever saw."

The dog's tail thumped now as he thought back with mixed emotions to the incident. Yes, he'd been rendered motionless from gluttony, and the gas pains had given him some bad moments for awhile, but on the whole the experience had been positive.

"Now, a bear'd eat that fifty-pound bag and ask you politely for another one," said Pinette.

Spatt gazed toward the window ruminatively. "Bears are deep."

"There ain't nothing so deep as a bear," agreed Pinette.

The bear took his time furnishing his apartment, because he wanted it to be in perfect taste. Light came from bubbling Lava lamps. A painting on velvet, of a trout, hung on the wall. The walls themselves were covered with a bright nursery paper depicting teddy bears playing with balloons. A beanbag chair, loosely molded to the bear's shape, was in front of a big-screen television set. He was seated in it now, watching a cartoon. A brightly colored coyote being struck with a wrecking ball and flattened to a shadow on a wall was very much to his liking. He turned on the lamp beside him, which had beads of illuminated oil that fell in a shower around a gold-tinted plaster Venus. The bear was especially fond of this object. This was because he was a bear.

After watching television for a short while, he became uneasy. He went to the kitchen and opened the refrigerator. It was filled with pies and cakes. "Do I have enough?" He was still troubled by the instinct to hoard, which he fought down by telling himself, "I can get more," and by reminding himself that the great thing about civilization was that you could always go shopping. Just to steady himself, he opened the kitchen cupboards and looked at his stores of honey. Every shelf was filled with the golden nectar, and there weren't any bees to contend with, another important advantage of city living.

He shuffled out of the kitchen and sat back down in front of the cartoon show. Now the coyote was being run over by a steamroller, his neck elongating as he tried to escape. The bear clapped his paws. "He won't get out of *that* one!" But he did get away, and the bear gave an appreciative growl. Coyotes were tricky. They'd stolen food from him a few times. You have to bang them against a tree real hard, which knocks the wind out of them. Then they behave.

These flickers of memory sank him into reflection about the forest he'd put behind him. "I should go back," he said to himself. But then he thought of his cupboard full of honey, and the web of forest reflections dissolved. He padded back to the kitchen and brought out a jar of tupelo honey. "This," he said as he admired its amber beauty, "is what it's all about."

He was jarred out of this meditation by the ringing of his telephone. He spun around in alarm, his claws spread to strike. When he detected nothing but the annoying sound, he stepped slowly from the kitchen into the living room and cautiously approached the phone. It was a child's phone in the shape of a pair of bunny rabbits, back-to-back, their ears holding the receiver. It had appealed to him in the store when he'd purchased it, but now he looked at it suspiciously, his eyes narrowing, his first impulse to hammer it, because bears are never at home to just anyone.

The bunnies continued to sound, their eyes lighting up with each ring; in the store he'd been delighted with this feature, but now the bunnies' eyes seemed to glow malevolently, on and off.

He removed the phone receiver from its cradle and set it down on the table. That shut the bunnies up, but now a voice was coming from the receiver.

"Hal, are you there? It's Zou Zou . . ."

Female, thought the bear to himself as he stared at the phone.

"Hal, I've been calling you for days . . . Hal? Are you busy? Are you writing? I'm not interrupting you, am I?"

He sniffed the earpiece, trying to get the scent of her, but it was no-go. However, as the voice continued to speak, he managed to place it. It was the female he'd rutted with. Cautiously, he lifted the receiver to his ear.

"Hal, I know you're there, I can hear you breathing . . ."

The bear felt the tiny voice spiraling down into his ear like a bee. He tapped the receiver into his palm, wondering if something might fall out of it, perhaps a tiny human female with pollen covering her legs.

"Hal, please talk to me. I'm back in Los Angeles and I'm trying to go about my life but I have to know how things stand between us."

The bear set down his jar of tupelo and untwisted the lid.

"Hal, please tell me what you're feeling. Do I mean anything at all to you?"

"Honey," said the bear as he removed the lid and admired the golden beads that dripped from it.

"Oh, Hal, I knew we weren't just a one-night stand. Hal, I'm prepared to make a complete commitment to our relationship. Do you feel that way too?"

"Sure," said the bear.

"Hal, I'm so glad I called. If you knew how I've been oscillating here. Staring at the phone, afraid to call, afraid I might be interrupting your writing, afraid of so many things . . ."

The bear listened to the female buzzing in his ear. He listened for quite a long time, fascinated by the droning little sound. But finally he said, "Well, good-bye," and hung up. He was pleased with the way he'd handled the telephone call. He'd been polite, but he'd said what was on his mind.

He picked up his honey jar again and tipped it to his lips. As the sweet ambrosia trickled over his tongue, he knew he was powerless against it.

"There's the feller we're looking for," said Pinette, pointing through the window of his truck toward a skinny individual walking by the side of the road with a stick in his hand and a burlap sack full of empty cans on his back. The afternoon sun was on him, and his shadow was long and strongly etched on the road. "Gus," called Pinette as he pulled his truck in beside the man. "Hop in."

The man raised his stick enthusiastically, then tossed it and the sack in back of the truck and climbed in. A sweet smell of soda emanated from his clothes. Pinette said, "Gus, this here's Art Bramhall. Him and me are writing a book together."

"Gus Gummersong," said the man, shaking Bramhall's hand.

Pinette steered the truck off the pavement onto a dirt road and followed it for several hundred feet, to a tiny shack. The yard surrounding it was piled with firewood, tires, scraps of iron, and a mound of soda and beer cans.

"By god, ain't this weather nice?" said

Gummersong, pointing with a grizzled chin toward the dead-calm afternoon sky. "Makes a man glad he ain't in jail."

Bramhall followed him into the smallest living space he'd ever seen. A tiny stove was at its center, with a narrow cot beside it. A pail of water with a dipper was on a stool, and a pair of pants hung from a nail on the wall. It was like being in a monk's cell—or an animal's den—and Bramhall felt strangely comfortable, more than he'd ever been in any of his own residences. "I like your place," he said.

"It keeps the flies off," said Gummersong modestly. His missing teeth gave him the look of a medieval fool. He moved the pail off the stool for Bramhall. Then he sat down on the cot and Pinette sat beside him.

The smell of the surrounding fields drifted in through the tiny window. "So tell me 'bout this here book you're writing," said Gummersong.

"Our first idea," said Pinette, "was to write about bears."

Gummersong reached beneath his cot, brought out a gallon jug in the crook of one thick finger. "Bear grease. Best place for a whoreson bear. In a jug." He unscrewed the lid and put the mouth of the jug under Bramhall's nose. The odor was overwhelmingly rank. "That's one bear we don't have to worry about."

Pinette took the jug and poured some of the grease on his finger and rubbed it into his boot. "The very best substance there is for turning water. Try 'er, Art."

Bramhall dipped a finger in the thick grease and rubbed it into his own boots, over the toes and into the seams. The smell filled the shack now and was somehow familiar to him, as if he'd known it for years.

Gummersong put the lid back on the bear grease bottle and held it up to a shaft of sunlight that came through his tiny window. Then he turned to Bramhall. "Here, you take 'er."

"I couldn't do that," said Bramhall, reluctant to reduce the few possessions of this hermit.

"You take 'er," chimed in Pinette. "There's all kinds of uses for bear grease."

Bramhall accepted the bear grease, cradling the jug in his lap. "Thank you, Gus."

"Don't mention it. Jug was taking up valuable space."

"As I was saying," said Pinette, "we're gathering stories for our book."

"Any money in the job?" Gummersong leaned forward keenly.

"Down the road," said Pinette.

Gummersong reached for the stick with which he speared empty cans and bottles. "It's al'uz down the road, ain't it."

"What I'm thinking," resumed Pinette, "is that we should write us a love story."

"In that case," said Gummersong, "you come to more or less an expert."

Pinette's bushy eyebrows went up and down several times expectantly, and he glanced at Bramhall to be sure he was paying attention.

"The love of my life," said Gummersong, "was a woman who bred guard dogs." He sighed and cradled his stick dejectedly. "She were easy on the eyes for a woman her age, and she set out a good feed for a man. But after awhile I noticed she took a few drops of something in her tea each night. I asked her what 'twas and she says arsenic. Claimed it settled her nerves, which it very well may have done, I never tried it meself."

"You told me," said Pinette, "it lent an air of tranquillity to the evenings."

"Well, it did," said Gummersong. "But she carried it too far. Started taking drops all day long and stiffened up at the dinner table one night. Knife in one hand, fork in the other. Couldn't move a muscle for over an hour. I told her the arsenic was having an adverse effect on her, and that she'd have to give it up. She knew better'n me, of course."

"Strong-willed," nodded Pinette.

"She had to be, in her line of work," said Gummersong. "Them guard dogs was mean sons-of-bitches.

Anyway, she said she had a nice income, and who was a damn fool man to tell her what to put in her tea?" Gummersong tapped the end of his stick thoughtfully on the rough board floor of the shack before resuming. "Well, a week later I found her facedown in the dog pen, and her nerves was more'n settled, she was croaked."

"Then Gus made his big mistake," said Pinette. "Any one of us mighta done the same."

"I lit out," said Gus, "and never asked myself what them dogs were gonna do when they got hungry. Course they et her."

"A hungry dog ain't particular," said Pinette.

"But they wasn't used to arsenic in their feed, and they keeled over dead themselves."

"When Gus come back here, the police wasn't far behind him."

"Said I'd poisoned her."

"Got into the papers and all," said Pinette admiringly. " 'Tain't every day a woman gets et by her dogs, with her boyfriend implicated."

"It took all the money I had to get clear of that case," said Gus. "Had to sell the farm. Even so, my reputation was tarnished."

"Well, you didn't have much of a reputation to begin with."

"True enough," said Gummersong. "Well, sir, when

all was said and done and the judge was bribed, I come out of it with barely the shirt on my back. I thrashed about for awhile, till I found my present line of work." Gummersong raised his stick again. "And I ain't never been happier. Got that whoreson farm off my back, and I spend my days the way I wants to."

"And he owes it all to that arsenic-eating woman," said Pinette as he got up to leave. "That's the part I think our readers will go for."

Gummersong accompanied them into the dooryard. "Don't be afeared to rub that grease in," he said to Bramhall.

"Thanks, I will," said Bramhall, swinging the jug by the handle. The thick yellowish liquid made a heavy sound. Though his literary life had been ruined by a bear, he lowered the jug with a sort of courtesy toward its contents. And a sort of acknowledgment came from it, that perhaps something was owed to him for his having been ruined by a bear and that the matter was being taken into hand.

Elliot Gadson and the bear stepped into the large, mirrored exercise room of Gadson's health club. The bear was in gym trunks and a T-shirt, as was Gadson, who'd suggested that his portly writer would benefit from working out. Gadson was himself in very good shape, having been a champion diver in his days at Yale. Currently he was being trained on the club's Nautilus equipment by Bart Manjuck, a powerfully muscled young man who awaited them now. Manjuck was eating a Bel Air Protein Wafer sold by the club and wore the club's own T-shirt, the sleeves of which were stretched tight around his biceps. His hand rested lightly on the tip of an upright metal bar on which was threaded a thousand pounds of circular iron weights.

"Bart," said Gadson, "this is my guest, Hal Jam."

"Nice to meet you," said Manjuck. "Ready for a little sweat?" He was gauging what kind of shape Mr. Gadson's friend was in. Grossly overweight, observed Manjuck. No muscle tone at all. And he's got a bad slouch. Looks like it takes all his strength just to stay upright. "I think we should start you out with a nice light program. Not too much weight, we don't want any strain."

"Fine by me," said the bear. No strain was just what he liked.

All around the room men and women were grunting and panting as they rowed and lifted and pedaled and climbed stairs that didn't go anywhere. Soon he'd be climbing stairs that didn't go anywhere either and then he'd be a full-fledged human. He was pleased to see how many females there were in the club. Maybe he could have them up for honey sometime. But when the eyes of the trim, pumping females fell on the porky-looking guy, they barely acknowledged his presence. They were building power bodies to go with their power jobs, and men who didn't keep themselves in condition were pathetic.

"Why don't you just step this way, Hal?" said Bart Manjuck. "I've got a curling machine free and we can put you on it with around fifty pounds resistance. That shouldn't stress you too much."

"Great," said the bear obligingly. As he followed Manjuck, he stubbed his toe on the pile of weights, so he picked up the weights to move them out of the way. "Okay?" he asked, holding the thousand-pound stack questioningly in the air. Bart Manjuck's head came forward like an astonished camel's. The trim women paused in their pumping and watched the porky guy pick up a second thousand-pound pile of weights in his other hand. Considerately, he took them to the corner of the room, where he set them gently down.

A petite middle-aged woman rose from her Nautilus machine and strode swiftly toward them. "You must introduce me, Elliot," she said in the throaty Southern accent that'd been heard on all the morning network shows that week. "Eunice Cotton," she said, extending her hand to Jam. "You're some power lifter."

"Well, of course, it wasn't a lift, strictly speaking," said Bart Manjuck, bouncing up and down on his Nikes and flexing his pectoral muscles.

Gadson said, "This is Hal Jam, Eunice. I sent you the manuscript of his book."

"*This* is Hal Jam? But I *loved* your book," she said. Though she hadn't actually read the manuscript, it had been on her desk for several days, awaiting a jacket quote from her, and she'd been getting a feeling for it each time she set her coffee cup on it.

Eunice's own books were about angels. Her latest, *Angels in Bed,* was written simply and beautifully for all the world, as was her last best-seller, *Angels in Business.* Her writing had the slow, easy flow of the bayou in it, and an alchemical inventiveness inherited from a father who'd spent his life turning cornmeal, water, and sugar into bootleg bourbon. Eunice had left the Louisiana swamps to become a hairdresser in New Orleans—a tarty-looking girl with nice high breasts and a ready laugh. One day, while breathing the fumes of a particularly strong hair spray, she had a vision of a strong, handsome, sexually pure male with frosted curls who said he was her guardian angel and that he was going to make her a star. Working in the evenings, she cranked out a two-hundred-page text on angels, written in the chatty style of a hairdresser talking to a client in curlers. Her word processor corrected her spelling and grammar, more or less, and she handed out copies of the spiral-bound manuscript at the American Booksellers convention in New Orleans. Elliot Gadson received the manuscript directly from Eunice, glanced at it, expecting something quaint or just plain crazy, and immediately saw the potential in Eunice's angels. He took Eunice aside to see if she was of reasonably sound mind and discovered that she was an authentic American yakker, a born distiller of dreams like her daddy, Anvil Cotton. She used too much corn and sugar in her mix, but it made for memorable moonshine, and made a fortune for Cavendish Press. Eunice moved to New York City, bought a seven-room apartment in the Dakota, and became a popular figure on talk shows. She shed her tarty look, assumed a pilgrimlike hairdo, dressed in dowdy clothes, and talked with Geraldo and Oprah, but underneath the dowdiness a sexy hairdresser was hidden; when she gave her throaty laugh or made some salty comment, the audience loved it.

93

Eunice stared at the burly young writer to whom she'd just been introduced. He resembled Daddy Anvil in his shape and unsuspected strength (Anvil could outrun government agents through a pitch-black swamp with barrels of booze strapped to his back). And there was something else about this man, something—well, angelic was the word. His eyes were cast shyly toward the floor, and he seemed unable to speak to her. Since her angelic revelation, Eunice had remained aloof from men, claiming that frosted-haired angels were woman's natural partners, but there was an otherworldly force coming off Hal Jam, as if he were comtemplating the invisible. He was, in fact, contemplating the smell coming from all the iron-pumping maidens in the gym. Strong stuff, he noted to himself. Makes a bear edgy.

Eunice took a sidelong glance at herself in the workout mirror. She'd been in the pool, which changed her pilgrimlike hairdo into a sleek cap that showed off the Cotton cheekbones and full lips, and Gadson was thinking to himself that maybe she was some kind of split personality, for the sensual woman in front of him was definitely not the prudish author of *Angels in Bed*, who wrote that the spiritual intentions of the winged beings should be realized through chastely imagined pillow fantasies. The imaginary angel would lie beside the reader through the night, in a feathery embrace that was thrillingly unconsummated.

"Elliot's the best editor there is," said Eunice to the bear when Gadson had mounted a stair climber to nowhere. "He discovered me when I didn't know jackshit about writing."

The bear shuffled uneasily from foot to foot. All around the room breasts bounced and thighs trembled, as if huge lady bears were trundling toward him on a forest path.

All these females could be mine, he said to himself. All I need to do is tear the place apart and hammer the piss out of the other males.

Might that be the wrong kind of exercise?

Possibly. Best to withdraw before I go wrong.

"Well, good-bye," he said, and turned toward the door.

Eunice Cotton hadn't chased a man since her last hairdressers' convention, and then she'd been plastered. Now she was the servant of an angel. At least she thought she was; sometimes she thought she was just crazy. Sometimes the voice of hairdressing inside her would say, *Eunice, you're rowing with only one oar in the water.*

"Isn't it a beautiful day? Fall is really here." She caught up to him on the sidewalk outside the health club. "Do you mind if I walk with you a ways?" Why, thought Eunice, I'm positively goin' after this fat man.

. . .

The head of a polished marble cherub was between them on the coffee table. It was one of hundreds of angels Eunice had in her apartment. Her collection ranged from fine antique European paintings to angels sculpted out of logs with a chain saw. A cheap wax angel with a wick in its head could move her as deeply as an angel painted by a Renaissance master. Sometimes her mood was lofty, and sometimes it was sentimental, and when it was sentimental you couldn't beat a plastic angel from Hong Kong. She'd set that little sucker right alongside her word processor and its sappy smile would get the inspiration flowing out of her, about how a woman can get plugged into angels and stay plugged in, no matter what kind of crap is going on in her life.

The bear was being cautious. His biological clock was already screwed up from rutting a female out of season. He'd been waking in the middle of the night and scratching on the walls.

Eunice sat back in her chair, between two tables, each of which held angel lamps, the winged creatures cast in bronze and supporting white shades, in which other angels floated, their bodies glowing softly. There was a life-size angel in one corner of the living room, painted in Easter-egg pastels and wearing one of Eunice's hats down over one eye. In the opposite corner was a Baroque masterpiece by Franz Schwanthaler, the figure's exquisitely carved wing tip sporting one of Eunice's umbrellas. The fireplace andirons were angels, and the oval mirror over the fireplace was held in the outspread arms of a gilt angel. A round marble-topped café table in the window had for its pedestal a muscular, scantily clad angel Elliot Gadson was particularly fond of. Angels supported other pieces of furniture throughout the apartment, smiling vacantly, like beautiful young men on tranquilizers. The bedposts were four angels, their bare feet seeming to float in the air. It was from the presence of these four handsome figures that Eunice had conceived her *Angels in Bed*. There were little magnetic angels in the kitchen, attached to the refrigerator, and others, shaped like jolly bowls, held utensils. In the bathroom a brass angel on the wall dispensed toilet paper. Another supported the soap dish in the shower, his aloof expression possibly meant to assure the bather that her naked form, glistening with bath gel, would not cause the angel to fall from grace. The bear was puzzled by all the angels surrounding him. He didn't know about angels, and thought he might have missed something about human beings, that maybe they came with wings they kept folded neatly out of sight most of the time.

Eunice put Rachmaninoff's *Vespers* on her disc player. She might be uneducated swamp trash, but she knew heavenly music when she heard it.

Human voices in potent musical combinations were new to the bear, and his ears rotated toward the sound. This was the inscrutable human essence, and it struck him hard. Humans were so complex, so mysterious, so rich in expression. What could a bear offer to compare with this?

Eunice saw him plugging in on a very high level. If she needed any further affirmation about his character, this was it. She was certain he heard angels too.

The bear closed his eyes as the sound enveloped him with its grandeur. Female voices rose, male voices descended, male and female blending in a weave of feeling that dwarfed his own crude emotion, his grunts and snorts of pleasure or discomfort.

"What are you thinking about, Hal?"

He opened his eyes and looked at her, then looked out her window toward the park and the buildings beyond it, on Fifth Avenue. The towers of light the human world had built seemed to be staring at him with innumerable eyes, like a sky full of owls. *When feeling insecure, attack,* said the ancient voice of his animal soul. He clenched and unclenched his paws. *Tear the place apart. You may not be as smart as humans but you're stronger than any of them.*

"I've been feeling tapped out myself lately," said Eunice, sitting down across from him. "I've done four angel books and I'll be goddamned if I can think of an angle for a new one. Everything a writer does is a sputtering candle, isn't it?" she asked, and as she said the words, recognized them as having come not from her, but from the angel within her. Hal Jam had called it forth. She just knew he had a bunch of high-level angels following him around.

The bear went to the window, his movements agitated. He'd stood on mountaintops and looked at vast tracts of silent wilderness, and felt his place in it. But what was his place in this city? All he had was an appetite, the simple, gobbling hunger of a brute.

The music soared where he couldn't follow. He felt like a mouse in a beehive. Mice like honey too, and sneak into a hive, not knowing the peril that awaits them. They're stung to death in the entranceway, attacked by the concentrated force of the bees. He was in the great human hive, listening to the hum from its countless rooms, where the human mystery was celebrated, and the human sting was held in readiness, to paralyze the intruder. His dark eyes lit up with anxiety, and he spun away from the window.

"Hal—"

He saw a tree and yanked it up by the roots, as bears will do when they get upset. The tree was an antique iron clothes tree shaped like an angel, and its roots were shallow but it still made an effective weapon. He swung it around, shattering the disc player with its music and the life-size plaster angel beside it. A second swing tangled him in the window curtains, which increased his panic. He raced around the room like a deranged Bedouin, trailing the curtains.

Eunice immediately grasped the situation. Her researches into angels had given her a shocking piece of news: demons were far more numerous than angels, as they could reproduce themselves sexually. The *Theatrum Diabolorum* of Martin Luther's time put the number of demons at 10,000 billion. How many more of the little sleazeballs were around now! And one of them had Hal Jam by the scruff of the neck. Having opened himself to the higher vibration, Jam had made it easy for the lower forces to enter. This good man was a prize for the archfiend Ahriman and his legions.

"Ahriman, cut the crap!" Eunice grabbed the end of the dangling curtain and yanked. The bear drew up short, caught by the throat, paws flapping at the air.

"I won't have trashy devils in my house," yelled Eunice. "You hear?"

The bear heard the *dangerous female* sound and reminded himself that male bears who ignore that warning can wind up minus a large patch of fur and skin. So he did what male bears do in such circumstances: he pretended he was looking the other way. Doing this while wrapped in a curtain was new for him, but he had to adapt. He picked up an angel paperweight and examined it with a show of interest.

"Out from this man, proud devil! In the name of Saint Michael, leave him in peace!"

The bear continued to pretend he always wore curtains while examining paperweights.

"Back into your pit, Ahriman, you tomcattin' piece

of filth!" Eunice was pleased to see Jam calming down, and it made her see how necessary it was for people to call upon the angels during temper tantrums, depressions, dark moods, in fact during all the instances of uncertainty and craziness that were invitations to Ahriman and his fiends. She reached for her notebook and pen.

"Well, good-bye," said the bear, taking off the curtain. Things had calmed down, and nobody'd sent for the zookeeper. He'd been upset about something but it was over now. He walked toward the door.

The shock is unspeakable, wrote Eunice, *when your husband suddenly turns violent. Is this the man I married? Could this be him, tearing down the curtains?*

The bear walked to the elevator and pressed the button. He did not reflect on the terror that'd gripped him only minutes before and the atrocious behavior he'd displayed. It'd happened but it wasn't happening now. That's all that matters to a bear.

You can forget about psychology, because it won't work. Because it isn't your husband. In fact, it's a devil. Eunice had her new book—*Angels in Your Arguments.*

"It's brilliant," said Gadson. He was seated in Eunice's living room, with Eunice beside him on the couch. They'd just read through the first two chapters of *Angels in Your Arguments,* with Rachmaninoff's *Vespers* playing in the background. "How did you ever think of it?"

"Hal Jam gave me the idea. Do you really like it?"

"I love it. We need a book like this, Eunice. I've ruined so many relationships with stupid, senseless bickering. An angel in the midst of all that would have been such a help." Gadson's eyes went to the Baroque angel in the corner, its pouting lips and naked arms and torso heartbreakingly reminiscent of a Cuban busboy who'd shared life with him recently. They'd quarreled bitterly over a soapy sponge, Gadson preferring to wash dishes with lots of hot water and very little soap. To think that I asked him to leave, that beautiful creature, over a sponge. "Yes, an angel is what we need, Eunice. That neutral third party we can turn to. You say Hal gave you the idea?"

"He's an angel in disguise," said Eunice. "His simplicity? His innocence?"

"Very unusual," admitted Gadson.

"But then you read his book—and I've read it now, every word of it—" Eunice pointed to the manuscript of *Destiny and Desire* on the coffee table. "—and you see that behind his innocence is a very old soul." She breathed a sigh for all the old souls like herself and Hal who had returned to earth during this troubled period. "We've become quite close."

"How close?"

"We have a deep spiritual bond."

"Come on, Eunice, this is your Aunt Elliot you're talking to. Are you sleeping with him?"

"We're beyond that."

"Nobody's beyond that."

"We have lunch together. We walk in the park." She gestured toward the fall foliage outside the window. "We hardly even speak. Somehow it's not necessary."

"He's tight-lipped all right," said Gadson. "But silence is not you, Eunice."

"He calms me. And I think I've helped him too. You know that Ahriman tries to possess him?"

"Ahriman?"

"The prince of evil." Eunice laid a hand on a statue of Saint Michael, mass-produced in Korea. "I called in the archangel to kick Ahriman's butt."

Gadson nodded thoughtfully. When he was with Eunice, he let his rational mind take a rest.

Eunice leaned toward him, the statue of Saint Michael in her hands. "You've heard Hal talk about traps and snares?"

"I've always found it odd."

"Traps and snares of the devil, Elliot. Hal knows he's being stalked by Ahriman."

"How chilling," said Elliot sympathetically, and looked around at the winged shadows on the walls. He thought of Eunice as a woman who'd sunk backward through several hundred years of evolution, and out had fluttered angels. They were medieval mental artifacts, he supposed, still frolicking around in the buried layers of the mind, still capable of influencing behavior, and that's why people bought her books.

"Ahriman is after everyone, Elliot."

"He'll never get us, darling." Gadson put his arm around his author and squeezed her shoulder. Then he pointed to the new manuscript. "You realize, of course, that *Angels in Your Arguments* leads directly to *Angels in Court?*"

Eunice clapped her hands. "Elliot, you're a genius!"

"When suing our neighbor, our employer, our spouse, our government, or a perfect stranger, the well-prepared litigant should always have an angel on the case."

"Since my last book, the fact that Frost used the word *like* as a simile .54 times per page is common knowledge." Dr. Alfred Settlemire of the University of Maine was riding in the automobile of his colleague from the English department, Bernard Wheelock. They were on a road that ran between large tracts of timberland, from which pulp trucks nosed out occasionally, loaded with spruce logs. "But," continued Settlemire as he stroked his goatee, "it isn't commonly known that he used *as if* .07 times per page. That's the substance of my new study on him. One needn't tell *you* the significance of this."

"Yes, yes, of course," said Wheelock enthusiastically, as he was junior man in the department, and Settlemire's study of *as ifs* was already under contract with a major university press. It was inconceivable to Wheelock that anyone gave a fuck about the number of times Frost used *as if*, but he knew he had much to learn about success.

"Temporal simultaneity, you see," continued Settlemire. "Crucial to grasping Frost. Which is where those .07 *as ifs* per page come in. Does one make oneself clear?"

"Absolutely." What Wheelock was most clear on was that cutbacks in the English department were anticipated now that government funding had fallen off. Settlemire, with his six-foot swaggering frame, his handsome head, and his *as ifs*, was a permanent fixture in the department. Wheelock's own position was shaky. But if Bramhall were out of the picture . . .

"How I wish Frost were still alive," said Settlemire. "I'd love to present him with my *as ifs*."

"I'm sure he would appreciate them."

"One feels connected to his spirit anyway," said Settlemire. "Diligence, perhaps that's the secret. Pouncing on the *as ifs*."

"I envy you that," said Wheelock, who had yet to pounce on anything.

"Your work is still gestating," said Settlemire kindly.

"I think this is Bramhall's road."

They took the winding unpaved road for several miles, to Bramhall's lane. "I wonder," said Wheelock, "if what we've heard about his health is true."

"Any man who sets out to make a deliberate copy of a best-seller is flirting with ethical fragmentation." Settlemire smiled a superior smile, but said no more, and Wheelock felt a peculiar mixture of apprehension and hope. The head of the English department had sent them out to reconnoiter the situation. Bramhall had been ignoring all department correspondence, and his sabbatical was over. Rumors were flying around about a mental breakdown. The head of the department had to know. The question in Wheelock's head was this: If Bramhall goes, will I replace him? Much as Wheelock had always liked Bramhall, he was hoping to find him dead or out of his mind.

They parked in front of Bramhall's cabin and got out. Settlemire knocked loudly on the door. The knock went unanswered. "Perhaps the fields?" Settlemire led the way, through the apple orchard, along a wagon path. "He's wasted his sabbatical, that much I can tell you. When I took my last sabbatical I worked, Wheelock. I counted *likes*. It was a grueling task, but one knew it was essential to any sort of understanding of Frost. Nowadays, of course, the computer does the counting. That's how Pettingzoo wrote his *Numbers of Nowhere in Wallace Stevens*. One's point is this, however—one must work. Not make a blatant copy of *Don't, Mr. Drummond*." Settlemire winged a stone into the woods with a smooth, graceful snap. "Modern American literature is Bramhall's field. He could have been counting *likes* in any number of authors. I've broken the ground. The way is clear. A new branch of critical thought has been opened. He could have had his place in that movement. But no. He chose otherwise."

Wheelock pointed toward the barn door. Bramhall

had just appeared in it, glancing furtively outward. Wheelock's heart leapt. *He's paranoid. Oh, perfect, perfect . . .*

They approached their colleague, and Settlemire called, "Bramhall, how are you?"

Bramhall eyed them in silence. Peculiar ideas were sprocketing along in his brain with a speed a mad inventor would envy. By some wonderful alchemy which he was hard-pressed to understand, his perception at this moment included the presence of a groundhog whose tunnel was near where Settlemire and Wheelock were walking. Bramhall felt the groundhog's uneasiness, even seemed to feel its thoughts—caution, suspicion—you never know who might shove a rat terrier down your hole.

Settlemire came up to Bramhall and extended his hand. "Good to see you, old man. One hears that you might be unwell."

"A bear stole my book."

Settlemire cast a quick glance toward Wheelock, of the sort attendants at mental institutions give each other when a new messiah is admitted to their floor. "A bear stole your book. Incredible. One didn't know bears did such things."

Bramhall caught the cynicism, but was not offended. His attention was on his subterranean acquaintance, the groundhog who was nervously enlarging his bolt-hole, that all-important escape hatch a prudent rodent must attend to. Just a precaution, said the shadowy voice in Bramhall's head, touch-up work mainly, mustn't be taken unprepared when the hostile snout comes calling.

Wheelock said, "We've all been concerned for you, Arthur."

Bramhall's nose twitched. The smell that was coming from Wheelock was ambition, a sweet greasy smell, as if Wheelock were roasting a pig in his shirt.

"The department was wondering if you've had trouble with your mail," said Settlemire.

"I don't open mail anymore."

"Ah." Wheelock was noting Bramhall's filthy pants. And he seems to be sprouting hair on his forehead. Glandular disturbance?

"Look here, Arthur, I brought along a copy of my *Qualified Qualifiers in Frost*. It's only a beginning but it points the way. Plenty of room for more research there."

Bramhall sniffed Settlemire's academic self-satisfaction, the smell of dead flies baking on an attic windowsill.

"One assumes you're finished copying best-sellers. All right, it didn't work out. A bear stole it, whatever, anything you like. We don't need an explanation. The point is, all is not lost."

"Maybe Arthur doesn't feel up to university work," said Wheelock hopefully. "We mustn't push him."

Bramhall turned away, into the sweet hay smell of

the barn. Its stout timbers, its sun-dried boards, its age, steadied him against these emissaries from his former life.

"Arthur," said Wheelock gently, "should we call a doctor?"

Bramhall lowered himself onto an old hay bale in one of the horse stalls and shook his head no. He envied the groundhog its bolt-hole, that secret place in which to vanish when unwelcome visitors disturb your tranquil meditation.

"I'm going to leave my book here on the hay," said Settlemire. Bramhall nodded again, aware that his silence was signaling the end of his life as a U Maine professor.

"We're going now, Arthur. We'll tell everyone you said hello. And give *Qualified Qualifiers* a glance. It might be just what you need."

The two professors left the barn and walked back across the field. "I'd say he's suffering a depression," said Settlemire. "Like Hamlet, you know. A world 'weary, stale, flat, and unprofitable.'"

"I think, perhaps, something a little more serious," suggested Wheelock, his glance falling on a whitened bone in the grass, of some creature whose days of roaming had ended, precisely here.

Back in the barn, Bramhall remained on his bale of hay, gazing at the smooth poles that formed the walls of the horse stall. There were patterns on one of the poles, left by some insect that'd burrowed along under the bark.

He traced the patterns, with the sense of reading the work of an alien calligrapher, whose life story was here. The script, though impenetrable, weighed more strongly with him than Settlemire's *Qualified Qualifiers*.

The rumble of a car sounded on the wagon road that led to the barn. Looking out the door, he saw the fur-bearing woman at the wheel. She drove to the barn, parked, and got out. The groundhog popped its head out of its hole and let out a long humanlike whistle. The fur-bearing woman turned toward it and smiled, then looked back toward Bramhall. "I love groundhogs. They're the only ones who ever whistle at me."

She approached the barn slowly. She'd heard that Arthur had begun living closer to the land, and this rumor had renewed her interest in him. She was wearing a heavy flannel shirt and jeans and carried a bunch of dried flowers. Entering the barn, she said, "I was picking herbs for winter and thought I'd bring you some." She'd woven dried flowers into her hair, and her voice was as sweet as the golden apples waiting to fall from the trees of the nearby orchard. As she sat down on the hay, her jeans pulled up slightly, revealing her hairy calves. Bramhall found them irresistibly attractive.

He lay in the hayloft of his barn with the fur-bearing woman beside him. Now that her flannel shirt was off he saw that she had fur under her arms too. She used no deodorant and an exciting odor enveloped him as she lifted her arms to unpin her hair.

Having expected cautious foreplay from the shy and timid professor, the fur-bearing woman was astounded when Bramhall spun her roughly around and bent her over.

"Arthur . . . my goodness . . ." Her personal space was being invaded too quickly. In fact, it'd just been filled up completely.

The little barn birds dived and twittered, feeling their nests of mud and sticks being shaken in the rafters. Oh, these clumsy humans, they're so heavy, and a nest is a delicate thing.

A growl rattled in Bramhall's throat. He bit the fur-bearing woman on the shoulder and felt an odd sensation at the tip of his coccyx, as if a tail were vigorously twitching there. Then he experienced the kind of orgasm the hero of his book had enjoyed, one that seemed to tap a huge reservoir of pleasure from deep inside the earth.

The fur-bearing woman's toes curled around the dry stalks of hay. When the tide of her own ecstasy subsided she looked back over her shoulder and saw Bramhall gazing at her. "You're a force of nature," she murmured, running her hand over his surprisingly burly chest.

The little birds swooped in and out of the barn, chattering to each other. Their nests were safe now but it'd been touch and go while the humans were humping.

"A bear stole my novel." Bramhall muttered his mantra up at the high ceiling of the barn.

"What do you mean?"

Bramhall did not immediately respond, as words no longer came easily to him. But finally a fragment surfaced from his life as a literature professor. "Shakespeare's *Winter's Tale*. Stage direction, act three, scene three." He stood, and without bothering to put on his pants and shirt walked to the barn door. "Exit, pursued by a bear," he said, and headed toward the woods.

"Arthur!" The fur-bearing woman, though a daughter of nature, was not prepared to wander the woods naked, especially in the cold. She hurriedly put on her clothes. "Wait for me!" By the time she reached the edge of the trees, Bramhall had vanished. The fur-bearing woman looked for a path but there was none. She felt as if she'd just been initiated into a frightening mystery of the forest. He'd said something about a bear stealing his novel, but what could that mean? Was he saying that his book had been channeled by a bear spirit? Did that account for his wild sexual performance? What secret power did this man possess? And what weekend seminar had given it to him?

The bear strolled through Greenwich Village in the bracing autumn air. A lovely night for a two-legged walk, he said to himself. Getting along like a real human being. Baseball hat, clip-on tie, comfortable shoes. What more could a bear ask for?

He was starting to enjoy crowds of people, with all their perfumed smells. His book had been purchased by Universal Studios for a million and a half dollars and Elliot Gadson had taken him to his own tailor, where several new suits had been made, one of which the bear wore this evening, a gray tweed which fit him perfectly. The tailor had expressed strong objections to the clip-on tie, but there are some points on which one can't compromise, reflected the bear to himself.

He entered Washington Square Park. The chess players were at their tables, and he paused to watch.

No one knows I'm a bear. Standing here, paws in my pockets. Just another hairy guy in the park. He walked on, with a lighthearted step. A young woman went by on roller blades, arms swinging briskly. I should get a pair of those, he thought to himself, a contemporary bear on the move.

Engrossed in watching the roller blader, he did not see the dog exercise area until it was too late. Dogs were chasing sticks and chasing each other and attempting various forms of intercourse. A male beagle came around a tree on the run, ears back, body low and almost flying. As he did so, he got wind of the bear. He skidded to a stop, stared for a moment, then threw his head back and let out the ancestral howl. It cut through the yapping and growling of the other dogs. It was the sound of the hunt. The other dogs took up the cry and raced to the fence, throwing themselves against it as they howled and barked, hackles up, teeth flashing.

The bear quickly changed course, pulling his baseball cap down over his head and trying to blend, but after a few anxious steps he reverted to bear-walking on all fours.

"Smoke, smoke," said a voice above him.

He forced himself to come upright, beside a man with matted hair and a ring in his ear.

"Grass, hash, crack," said the Jamaican entrepreneur, falling into step beside him. "What you fancy, mon?"

"Potato chips," said the bear with a nervous look back toward the dogs.

The entrepreneur frowned. He did not have time to waste. He worked hard each day the American way, to buy big cars and little phones. "I got California sensamilla, mon."

"Do you have pretzels?"

The entrepreneur's eyes flashed angrily. Image was important in the park and he could not afford to be joked around. He jabbed a finger into the bear's chest. "Hey, don't be jiving me, mon, or I stick you in the guts."

The bear's eyes darted fearfully in the direction of the howling dogs and he moved away hurriedly, out of the park. Dogs had the power to unmask him, to turn him into a raging, desperate animal forced to make a stand in public, where he'd quickly be arrested and taken away to the zoo. I let my guard down, he said to himself. I got cocky. Remember what Bettina said, you're not a star until they can spell your name in Karachi.

He continued through the Village, toward Gadson's loft in SoHo. He'd visited it once before and the smells of its restaurants and shops formed a map in his brain, which he was following now, from Greek food to Italian food to Chinese food. At the entrance to Gadson's loft building, he smelled the Clinique face scrub which Gadson used. He rang the bell and then climbed the stairs, toward a cloud of perfumes and colognes and the sound of voices.

"Hal, so glad you could make it." Gadson met him at the door and showed him through a corridor hung with turn-of-the-century posters of gay nightspots—Little

Bucks, the Artistic Club, the Black Rabbit of Bleecker Street where the French Fairy had put on his remarkable floor show. There was a blown-up page from *The New York Herald* of 1892 describing activities at a Greenwich Village nightclub called the Slide where "Orgies Beyond Description" took place. The bear studied the posters, struck by the men in their evening attire, with canes and capes. He'd have to talk to Elliot about getting a cape.

Gadson was leading him into the main room of the loft, whose entry was decorated with tall ferns in slender vases. Converted gas lamps illuminated the walls, and the furniture was Victorian. The guests were mostly from the literary world, and had already heard rumors about Hal Jam's forthcoming book and the sale to Universal. "He does look like Hemingway," said more than one person, though some said it was just a superficial impression, not a true likeness.

Bettina appeared like the queen of the bumblebees, her gold and black dress clinging to her buzzing little figure, and her eyes bulging with the feverish fires that ruled her. Her path through the room was erratic, for she wanted to be everywhere at once. A tortilla chip attached itself to her flying scarf as she pivoted past the buffet table, and Chum Boykins removed it with a compulsive nip of his fingers.

Bettina waved to Eunice Cotton and joined her in a corner of the room. *Angels in Bed* had now sold a million copies, and Eunice was everlastingly grateful for Bettina's genius. Bettina had toured her heavily in Bible Belt country, and sales had soared, because Bettina had included a cute young male stripper on the tour. She'd had the stripper wear a short white tunic and gaze with impartial love at the ladies while Eunice read from *Bed*. During the book-signing session afterward, the muscular angel was especially attentive to Eunice, fussing over her, whispering to her, all of it stage-managed by Bettina, to give the impression of what angels actually did for people. Turnouts for the readings had been high, and the angel was now making promotional visits on his own to shopping malls. Gadson had signed him up to write his autobiography, tentatively titled *Tarnished Wings*.

"Hal Jam is here," said Bettina to Eunice excitedly. "I was afraid he wouldn't come."

"That man is a saint," said the angel writer.

"Can we go quite that far?" asked Bettina.

"He's above it all, Bettina. You told me yourself he doesn't care about publicity."

Bettina had to admit this was true, to her great puzzlement. She'd known writers who were indifferent to politics and even to sex, but she'd never met one who was indifferent to publicity.

Eunice tilted her head back slightly and closed her eyes. "It happens the minute Hal Jam appears. I'm hearing my angel."

"What's he saying?" asked Bettina with real interest. She desperately wished she had an angel but she knew she'd never qualify. She felt like the remains of a broken travel agency, had sent too many people off on trips peddling books. Her eyes swiveled to the door. "That's Zou Zou Sharr walking in. Do you know her? She's a killer Hollywood agent."

"I used to do my hair that shade of red," said Eunice. "I used to do a *lot* of people's hair that shade."

Bettina zipped across the room and slipped her arm through the bear's. "There's someone I'd like you to meet. If he likes your work it could help enormously."

She introduced him to Kenneth Penrod, professor of English at Columbia and the author of *The Decline of Literature*. Penrod found the bear unusually taciturn and liked it. Penrod waited, wineglass in hand, as the bear struggled to express what was on his mind, glancing in the direction of Washington Square Park with haunted eyes. Finally the bear said, very slowly, "I've heard the howling of the dogs."

The depth of feeling in the bear's voice was not the idle stuff Penrod generally heard at functions like this. "I know exactly what you mean," answered Penrod. "Our literary values are being totally corrupted by men like Ramsbotham over there." He pointed to the other prominent critic in the room, Samuel Ramsbotham of NYU, whose book *The Literary Revolution* had been outselling

Penrod's two to one. "Dogs? You're absolutely right. They're howling at our door."

The bear's gaze shot toward the door of the loft, and the ridge of muscle at his neck swelled. "I hate dogs."

"There's always one or two who show up, usually with an entourage of sycophants." Penrod cast another disdainful glance toward Ramsbotham.

The bear's neck muscles quivered. "I'll tear them apart."

"I hope you do." Penrod was impressed. This man Jam lived his beliefs. So rare. So very, very rare. "I'm eager to read your novel, of course. I've heard a great deal about it already from Bettina and Elliot."

The bear nodded, but his eyes kept returning to the door, and then to the window. His indifference to talking about his own book further impressed Penrod. He's not consumed by ambition, reflected the critic. He's concerned, as I am, about the crisis in literature. "I think you might get something out of my *Decline*," said Penrod. "I'll have the publisher send you a copy. It's pioneer work, of course, but there are *some* points with which you'll be in sympathy."

"How are you two getting on?" asked Bettina, returning in a whirlwind and spilling champagne into Penrod's vest pocket, where it gave a good soaking to his heirloom pocket watch.

"Oh god, Ken, I'm sorry," said Bettina, trying to soak up the spilled champagne with her scarf.

"Quite all right, Bettina," said Penrod. "You've been spilling things on me for years. I look upon it as something of a ritual."

The bear went to the window of the loft, looking anxiously in the direction of Washington Square, through which he could never walk again. "Dogs," he said to himself.

"What about them?" asked Gadson, coming up alongside him.

The bear struggled to say more, but couldn't express the nuances of a hostility that was ancient. "Talking is hard."

"I know," said Gadson. "I was three years old before I spoke a single word. I had the words in my head, but I was making sure of my listeners." They moved at the edge of the crowd, along a library wall that was lined with Gadson's collection of first editions. "Books were always my best friends. As I'm sure they were yours. You were raised in a rural area, and I don't suppose you saw many people."

"I saw a man through a window."

Gadson was at a loss. "And did you get to know him?"

"I hung around," replied the bear, trying to express his memory of the time, because human beings did that, they talked about things that'd happened to them. The past is unimportant to a bear, but he wanted to become human, so he attempted to describe it. "He had something I wanted."

Gadson wondered: Was Jam's peculiar shyness simply a matter of him not being able to come out of the closet? He drew Jam to the end of the room, near a painted screen that framed the doorway, the screen depicting two Japanese sailors and another man, in shadow, along a waterfront.

"I wanted his meat," said the bear. "He left it around."

"You wanted . . . his meat?"

"I couldn't help it."

"And?"

"I grabbed it."

Gadson suddenly saw it all, a warm summer afternoon, and the unknown man stripped to the waist, possibly tossing hay around, sinews rippling. It sounded idyllic.

"Meat," repeated the bear, remembering more clearly the hunk of venison he'd romped off with. "Sweet buck meat."

"How frankly you put it, Hal."

The bear's long tongue came out and lapped over his snout. "Tasty."

"Hal, my dear friend, if you ever feel the need of another . . . hunk of meat . . ."

The bear was pleased by the seriousness with which his editor treated the subject of meat. He put his paw on Elliot's shoulder. "You understand."

"Oh, I do, Hal, I do. I understand completely." This unexpected kinship with Jam gave Gadson a warm glow. They'd risked intimacy and had found a new footing. "But will you ever write about this? Because with your touch, it could be beautiful. It could be your next book."

"The next book . . ." The bear's forehead creased in a frown.

"Don't force it, Hal. It'll come."

"I can't find it."

"It could begin with your seeing that man of yours through the window. We need a book like that, Hal. Just think if Hemingway had told us what his sex life was really like."

Zou Zou Sharr appeared, coming hesitantly toward them. There were other people in this room she should be chatting up, but she only wanted to be with Hal. Gadson stretched out his hand to her, and she stepped under a star-shaped lamp with them, its beams of light falling onto her power hair. "How are you, Elliot?" she asked, but her eyes were on Jam's, looking for a sign of his affection.

The bear sniffed the female. It was the female he'd

rutted with, which meant she was his Hollywood agent who'd sold his book for a million and a half dollars. He smelled her desire. Very good stuff, he said to himself. Light. Exquisite. Indirect. Not the heavy, knockout odor you get from female bears, who leave their scent hanging in thick clouds in the woodland corridors. It shocked him to remember that his heart used to race when he encountered that coarse smell; one whiff of it and he'd start to search frantically around for the direction it was coming from, ready to kick the ass of any other male who was following it too. Human females laid their rutting scent down so much more subtly, spraying other scents on top to make it harder to identify. And then covering it all with frilly panties. That was evolution. Lady bears had such a long way to go they'd probably never be wearing frilly panties.

"I must leave you two for awhile," said Gadson with a glance toward newly arriving guests.

"Hal, I've missed you so terribly," said Zou Zou as soon as Gadson withdrew. She pressed herself against Jam. The incredible power of his lovemaking, she said to herself, has drawn me across the continent. That and several deals which I need for my retirement, I mustn't forget the deals, I should be working the room, but god I can't stay away from this *man*.

The bear's back was tired. He wished he were home watching cartoons. He would make his polite good-byes now, and go. He put out his hand to the female. "Well," he said, "good-bye."

"Hal, please, you can't say that."

"I can't?"

"No, you simply can't."

Confused, he tried another of the forms of good-bye he'd learned. "How about—up your ass?"

Zou Zou was momentarily taken aback by his suggestion, then gave a sudden squeeze to his paw. "If it's what you want, darling."

The bear turned and walked away, with Zou Zou walking beside him. "Are we going?" she asked. "Right now?"

"You bet," said the bear. He walked toward the door of the loft, a movement that was quickly noted by Gadson and Bettina.

"Well," said Gadson, "she beat me to it."

"It wouldn't have worked for you, Elliot," said Bettina. "He's not *that way.*"

"Great sportsmen are *all* a little that way, dear."

"Penrod likes him."

"Well, Penrod's *certainly* that way." Gadson hurried to say good-bye to his writer, joining him and Zou Zou in the hallway. "Good night, Hal, let's do lunch this week."

"Sure," said the bear, who liked the way humans made plans to eat together, in the certain knowledge that food would be there when they arrived. He descended the stairs, thinking about it, how they had food everywhere, waiting. Bears could not do this.

"Such a crisp, cold evening," said Zou Zou as they stepped onto the sidewalk. "Can we walk a little?"

The bear sniffed the air for dogs, but there were none in the immediate vicinity. There was dogshit around, of course. There was dogshit all over Manhattan. Dogshit was the dominant smell in the city. Dogs had staked a very large claim in the human world with their crap. He understood that it was necessary for reference purposes, but they'd carried it too far.

Zou Zou was taking sidelong glances at him as they walked, her heart still waiting for a real acknowledgment from him. "It's been too long," she said, trying to prod him a little. "And too far. At nights I wake up staggered by the physical distance between us."

The bear nodded with only vague understanding and still vaguer interest. Events mattered if they hit him in the face. Things at any distance lacked reality. What was real at the moment was his hunger. He shouldn't have left the party without eating his fill; now he'd have to eat on the move, and there weren't any restaurants on this block. Maybe he could catch a rat. Or even a handful of ants, which had a nice, vinegary flavor.

"I know we each have our work," said Zou Zou, "but at the moment I'm just going through the motions in my job. Because all that's on my mind is you. Am I admitting too much? But why should I hide what I feel? We don't have time for that."

The bear had no idea what this meant either. He was thinking that potato chips were a big improvement on ants, but ants were still okay.

Zou Zou suddenly felt that perhaps she *had* gone too far. She didn't want to frighten him off by clinging. And so, she thought to herself, once again I'm completely disoriented in a relationship. "I don't mean that I expect anything from you, Hal. You're a catalyst, yes, but it's actually a matter of how I feel about myself. You've given me a new direction. I'm not just talking about sex, though of course that's been an eye-opener too. But I've started to take some of your values as my own and they suit me very well. For example, your scorn of the social contract and the way you live in the moment. Why shouldn't I live that way too?"

"Pretzel!" said the bear with the sudden enthusiasm she'd hoped would have greeted the honesty of her admission. He was pointing excitedly at a vendor's wagon up ahead and she was hurt and angry until she caught the gleam in his eye and realized he was, as usual, showing her how to be the way she wanted to be, spontaneous and free. "Yes, of course," she said with a smile, "let's have a pretzel."

He purchased pretzels for them and they walked on, Zou Zou slipping her arm through his. "You have a way of puncturing pomposity, Hal. I need that."

"A good pretzel."

"Yes, it is, it truly is," she said as she slipped it into her purse, "but I think I'll save it for later."

"I like salt."

"Life's flavor," said Zou Zou. "I understand, Hal, I truly do."

As they walked, the bear checked under every tree for briefcases containing manuscripts.

"You look pensive," said Zou Zou, observing his downward gaze. She felt certain now that her mention of her real feelings must be bothering him. Was he just another man who was unable to commit? "I don't want you to feel trapped."

"Trapped?" The bear looked at her in alarm, then snapped his head toward the shadows. "Are there traps?"

"Hal, there are always traps."

"Where are they?" He sniffed the air for the smell of meat and steel.

"Don't worry. I didn't set one."

"But somebody else might have." His head moved slowly back and forth as his nose swept the air.

"What do you mean?" asked Zou Zou quickly. "Are you seeing someone else?" She knew he had lunch with Eunice Cotton, supposedly just friendly lunches. But could that angel-flogging bitch be trusted to keep her hands off a catch like Hal? "Hal, I think I have the right to know. Who else are you seeing?"

"Well," he said, "I see Elliot."

"You do?" A stab of pain and fear went through her. She knew Hal was raucous in bed but she hadn't thought he was bisexual. "Do you take—precautions?"

"What are precautions?"

Am I at risk? wondered Zou Zou, hoping that Elliot had the good sense to be careful. But of course he would be, he had to be, although men can be insanely reckless when they get excited. "Do you . . . enjoy yourself with Elliot?"

"We have a pretty good time."

"What do you do?"

"Just the usual things."

"The usual things," echoed Zou Zou, dumbfounded by the triangle she was now part of. How naive I am, she said to herself. That first night at the Plaza, when he was so reluctant—now I understand. "Hal, we can talk about this. What is your real sexual orientation? Men or women?"

"Pretzels." The bear looked back over his shoulder. The strong smell of horse sweat was reaching his nose, and then he saw a policeman on horseback, turning the corner toward him.

The policeman's gloves were immaculate; his riding

boots gleamed; he rode with machismo, and his horse was a machismo horse. It liked shitting in conspicuous inter-sections, after which it strutted proudly. It was strutting proudly now, having dropped a splendid load in front of a prominent art gallery, farting loudly for good measure. Both horse and rider cast a contemptuous look at the bear. What's that fucking meatball doing with that good-look-ing broad? wondered the mounted policeman. C'mere, baby, I'll give you something to ride.

Him and me both, lady, said his macho horse. But then the horse received a most unsettling scent up his big flat nose. *Am I getting this right?* he wondered, and froze. The policeman urged him forward with a John Wayne kick as the horse took another deep sniff. He had been trained to remain calm in crowds, to ignore gunfire and gushing water mains, but the NYPD equestrian training manual had never covered Bear In The Street. The horse's brain was firing off hoary images of horses being eaten by bears and—this was a nice touch from the horse's collective unconscious—then the bears would roll the empty horsehides up into a nice neat ball and deposit them as a territorial marker. The horse whinnied and reared back on his hind legs, with visions of his guts being ripped out. The policeman struggled with the reins as the horse bucked and reared again, hooves beating the air in terror. The mounted policeman bounced up and down in the saddle and his manly boots lost their grip inside the manly flapping stirrups. *This can't be happening,* he said to himself as he felt himself sliding backward out of the saddle and then, as the horse bucked again, sliding off the horse's rear, clutching at its tail. He fell in a heap on Spring Street and scrambled to his feet, trying to pretend he'd deliberately leapt backward from the saddle in a trick dismount, but his helmet was in his eyes and his horse was galloping away.

"That poor man," said Zou Zou.

"This way," said the bear, moving her in the opposite direction.

"But he might be hurt."

"This way," repeated the bear, for the mounted policeman was giving him an angry look.

"What is it, Hal?" asked Zou Zou softly.

"The zoo," said the bear.

"It *is* a zoo out here, but you haven't got anything to hide from the police. Or do you?" Now that she knew he swung both ways sexually, she suspected he might be into other shadowy things.

The bear hurried them along for many blocks until he got an entirely new smell, of sesame oil and incense and large amounts of stored grain. A pagoda-shaped telephone booth appeared. They were in a neighborhood he'd never explored. He was delighted with the appearance of little winding streets, which were forestlike in their turns and shadows. The smells continued to fascinate him, of fresh fish and pressed duck, and the heavy, smoky odors of restaurants. Zou Zou felt her mood change with his as they strolled through the jumble of sights that was Chinatown. So he swings both ways, she thought to herself, so what? I enjoy life when I'm with him. I have a pretzel in my purse. I'm breaking free of restraint.

They went from window to window, examining the tiny worlds displayed there, of jade monkeys and paper flowers, red silk lanterns and antique coins. And then the bear froze. They were looking in the window of a Chinese pharmacy at bins of gnarled roots and dried berries. Beside the bins was a row of bottles, and every bottle had the portrait of a bear on it. The bear squinted, reading slowly. "Gall bladder . . . of . . . *bear?*" He drew back in horror.

"Hal—" Zou Zou had to hurry after him, through the little winding street.

Gall bladder of bear, thought the bear as he ran, his arms pumping, his legs churning. Not good. Not good at all.

As he ran he looked right and left, at humans in doorways. He could hear their thoughts: *Wait for bear come along, cut out gall bladder, grind into pills. Take two every hour.*

He raced out of the little side street, onto the Bowery, and waved his paw for a taxi. A man walked past, looking at him. *Know any bear? Bring around. We put gall bladder in bottle.*

Not mine you won't! Not Hal Jam's gall bladder!

The bear roared for a taxi, then stopped himself, realizing he was roaring like a bear. Calm down, articulate slowly. "Tax-iii," he said in the most genteel voice he could manage, just as Zou Zou caught up with him.

"Hal, where are we going?"

"Tax—iiii," he called again, wanting to get out of this part of town immediately.

"Something in that window upset you. What was it?"

A taxi pulled toward them, and the bear jumped in. Zou Zou climbed in after him. He was looking out the back window apprehensively.

My god, wondered Zou Zou, is he going to crack the way Hemingway did? Or is he on some weird drug? And if he is why doesn't he give some to me?

Gall bladder of bear, thought the bear. This is the real human world. They act civilized, they wear frilly panties, but when they feel like it, they'll put you in a bottle.

"You know what I think, Hal?" said Zou Zou. "We should go dancing. You need to forget yourself a little." She gave the driver the address of a midtown club, and the cab shot into traffic.

The bear's head moved back and forth slowly as he fought his animal fears. He'd risked a great deal to get his book published and he mustn't cave in now. But he was having another identity crisis, with nothing to hold on to in the human or the animal world. Nothing but . . . this woman with the nice legs. He liked legs that weren't hairy. He liked smooth-shaven legs. Wasn't this a sign of his growing humanity?

"Hal, how sweet . . . but not in the back of a taxi . . ." She pushed his paw down out of her skirt. The bear tried again, running his paw along the soft, comforting flesh of her thigh.

"Please, Hal, don't be an animal."

He recoiled from her. "I'm not an animal!"

"Well, no, of course you aren't." She saw she'd hurt him and she tried to repair the damage, pressing her leg gently against his. "I appreciate your attentions, but—" She nodded toward the driver on the other side of the protective grill. "—we have to wait until later."

The bear didn't understand about the driver. He only knew he was cracking, and tried to calm himself. I'm riding in a taxi in Manhattan. How many bears can say that?

"Hal, darling, please don't be offended." Zou Zou was concerned that she'd ruined the momentum of a feeling, one that came from a great writer who also happened to be the most amazing lover she'd ever had. "I acted like a fool. Here . . ." She put his paw on her thigh, on the lacy tops of her nylons. "But slip this on, it's just a precaution." She straddled the bear, her skirt climbing above her thighs.

The bear was still panicked, but Zou Zou's caresses slowly quelled his fears that he was no one at all. If he were no one at all, her legs wouldn't be wrapped around him the way they were. Rutting with a human female definitely made you feel like you were someone. Maybe that's why human beings did it so much. "I'm someone," he said.

"Yes, Hal, yes, you are. And I'm an agent. It's so difficult sometimes. I'm always thinking about deals. I forget the pulse of *life*. Oh . . . oh . . . ohmygod I can't believe this is happening . . . in a taxi . . ."

A roar of pleasure escaped the bear's throat. Zou Zou bounced up and down, driven by passion and the pockmarked pavement which tossed the cab around. "Hal . . . you're magnificent . . ." She loved him. There. She'd admitted it. She moved more rapidly, her jealousies and confusion about him dissolving in the heat that was spreading through her body like the rapture of a successful deal. She gasped, and bumped her head on the ceiling of the cab, then collapsed on his shoulder. Never in my life, she thought to herself. Never anything even close.

The bear closed his eyes, at peace with himself again, his dissociation over. He'd passed a great human milestone. He'd done it more than once a year.

135

"Hal . . . I feel totally . . . what am I trying to say . . . completely . . . *fulfilled*." Deal memos were cross-firing in her mind, with fantastic sums attached to them. "You took me out of myself," she explained as she slowly rearranged her underwear and fixed a strand of her long auburn hair into place. She wanted to just lie in his arms, but they were nearing their destination. She saw he was having trouble with his zipper and fixed it for him. "You're a wonder."

"I'm someone," said the bear.

The cab deposited them in front of a small Latin nightclub. Zou Zou stood on the sidewalk with the bear, straightening her skirt. When she was satisfied with her repairs, she led them into the club. She'd been there for the premiere party of a dance film her agency had packaged, and the owner made a show of giving them the best table in the house, which it wasn't, and then gallantly kissed Zou Zou's hand.

The bear gazed in fascination at the dancers. Couples glided past him, their bodies separating and entwining with the sensuality of summer in the forest, the males aggressive and the females suggestive as the rhythm of the music drove them on.

Zou Zou led him to the floor, into the big-band Latin sound. She knew the steps, her lead was strong, and the bear was drawn into her movements. His own steps were tentative at first, but then the ancient ability of the dancing bear surfaced. He heard the slower pulse within the music and took the lead. His steps were dainty and carefully measured. His huge barrel frame had a peculiar majesty and suddenly he was the focal point for the band, for they realized he had *it*. The other dancers soon became aware that an original talent was on the floor, with a style that was commanding, yet easy, almost indifferent.

"Hal, I had no *idea*—" Zou Zou had never had a partner so elegantly understated. He moved with such dignity, his slow grace broadcasting itself to the other dancers, who watched him with appreciation. His nimble turns, executed on such bulk, were enormously sexy. Zou Zou saw the other women eyeing him. He didn't need to posture or project an attitude; his authority declared itself discreetly and was much greater for it. In summers past, on the forest floor, he'd strutted, his roar shaking the trees. Somehow this made itself felt in the maneuvers he executed now, to the trill of the trumpets and the beat of the drums. One of the other dancers said to his partner that he recognized this guy, that he was an Argentine tango master who loved to eat; one of those giants who knew how to live. And these New York dancers, as fiercely competitive as any in the world, accorded him the greatest honor—they gave him room, so he could shine.

When the dance ended, the bear and Zou Zou made their way toward their table, through a shower of compliments which left no doubt as to the esteem in which the bear was held. Zou Zou, being in possession of him, came in for comment too, something that'd never happened to her on a dance floor. Hal Jam was becoming more to her every moment. Their casual affair had taken on a significance she hadn't anticipated. She suddenly knew that he was going to break her heart and she even knew how, through that reserve he always kept, which she now realized was bolstered by an immense dignity. All of this was what made him the writer he was, and she understood, with a jolt, that on the dance floor just now she'd seen his enormous capacity for self-expression. His appearance on the literary scene was no accident; he was a natural, as Hemingway had been. And as with Hemingway, his celebrity was inevitable. This coming fame would only distance him from her, and the irony was that she would help to create it.

Arthur Bramhall sat with Vinal Pinette and Gus Gummersong in Gummersong's shack. Pinette's dog was lying in the yard, watching a chickadee pecking seeds from Gummersong's feeder. From across the frozen field came the sound of a chain saw, whining like a large metallic bug. Bramhall, like the dog, was gazing at the bird, and like the dog he experienced the fleeting mental image of having the bird in his mouth and crunching on its tiny bones.

"Something very peculiar is happening to me," he said to Gummersong and Pinette.

"What you need," said Gummersong, "is to move in with a woman. Nothing like a woman to change a man's outlook."

The sound of the chain saw stopped. The air was still, except for the chirping of the chickadee.

"But look at my arms," said Bramhall. "They're enormous."

"They have bulked up some," said Pinette.

Bramhall put his hand around an iron stove poker. "I feel like I could bend this over my head."

"I'd ruther you wouldn't," said Gummersong politely.

Bramhall listened to the scurrying of a mouse beneath the floor of the shack, and the rhythmic slither of the snake that was stalking it. The mouse bit daintily on a morsel of grain. The snake bit deftly on the mouse.

"Homer seems to be done cutting," said Pinette, gazing out across the field at an approaching figure.

Homer strolled toward the shack and peeked in at the door. "S'pose I could get a lift into town, Vinal?" he inquired nonchalantly.

"Sure enough, Homer. Where you bound for?"

"Thought I might visit the hospital," said Homer, pulling a handkerchief out of his pocket. In the handkerchief was a toe. "Ran the chain saw through my boot."

"What'd you plug the wound with?" asked Gummersong.

"Pine needles and sap."

"The very best," said Gummersong. "I've seen some dandy mutilations in my day and pine needles and sap was al'uz what we stuffed them with."

"I'd been meaning to buy steel-toed boots," said Homer sociably as they walked across the yard toward the truck. "But one thing and another come along, and I just never did."

"Doesn't pay to rush into a purchase," said Gummersong.

They climbed into the truck, Homer and Bramhall

up front with Pinette, and Gummersong in the open back with Pinette's dog. As the truck bounced over the dirt road, Homer laid his precious bundle on the floor and turned to Pinette. "How've things been with you, Vinal?"

"Can't complain," said Pinette. "And yourself?"

"Oh, pretty good," said Homer, apparently not counting the recent severing of his big toe. Listening to the two men, Bramhall felt something in himself that echoed their stoicism. It was brand-new and seemed to come from his feeling of animality, an acceptance of life as the beast accepts.

The truck roared along the winding country road. A river kept pace with them, sparkling on their left. Homer probed the tip of his boot. "Bleeding 'pears to have stopped."

"Pine needles and sap," said Pinette, nodding. "I wounded a bear one time, and that son-of-a-whore plugged *his* wound with pine needles. And I never did catch him."

"A bear is cunning," agreed Homer.

"One stole Art's suitcase."

"That a fact?" asked Homer with interest. "Get anything valuable?"

"Not very," said Bramhall, who felt that in the *lost-objects* category, Homer's toe far outweighed his novel.

The truck hit a hole in the road and all three men

bounced up in their seats, striking their heads on the roof of the cab. "Bad job on the road this year," said Pinette. "The patching tar just didn't seem to hold."

"There's a way of putting in that tar," said Homer sagely. "You got to clean the hole good, and then you got to layer your material."

A rapping came on the back window of the cab. Bramhall turned. Gummersong was signaling for them to stop.

"What the hell's he want?" asked Pinette.

"He's pointing to the side of the road," said Bramhall.

"Probably wants to stop for a soda can," said Pinette. "We'll catch it on the way back."

Gummersong continued to shout above the roaring of the truck. He was struggling to keep his balance as he pointed toward the road. Finally he yanked off his boot and pointed at his big toe, then pointed to the road again. Bramhall looked down at the floor of the cab. "Excuse me, Homer, but where's your toe?"

Homer reached down, then peered around, under the dash and under the seat. "Appears to be gone."

"Gone?" inquired Pinette.

"I guess she went out through the floorboards," said Homer with unchanging placidity. "You got a few good-size cracks down here, I see."

Pinette pulled the truck to the side of the road,

turned around, and called back to Gummersong. "Where'd we lose 'er, Gus?"

Gummersong leaned forward around the cab, pointing. "Just by that there hydro pole, the one that's tilting." Gummersong, for whom the side of the road was as familiar in all its details as his own face, kept a trained eye out as they drove back along the road. "There, on the edge of the pavement."

Pinette eased the truck to a stop, the front wheels of the truck on either side of the toe. "Go get 'er," he said to Gummersong.

Pinette's dog leapt out of the truck ahead of Gummersong and dove under the front bumper. He snapped the toe up in his jaws, chewed it twice to get the flavor of the thing, and then swallowed it.

Nice and tangy, he remarked to himself. Just a hint of salt in it. He came out from under the bumper, tail wagging.

"Vinal," said Gummersong, "your dog et 'er."

"Et what?"

"Homer's toe."

Pinette flung open the door and jumped down. The dog looked at him proudly, having handled the incident well, he thought.

"You stupid son-of-a-whore." Pinette slapped his hat at the dog, who darted quickly aside. Bramhall and Homer climbed out of the truck.

"He et your toe, Homer," explained Pinette contritely.

Homer looked at the dog. The dog's tongue was out, his tail still wagging. He was unused to this much attention and, lowering his head between his paws, he began barking enthusiastically.

Homer gave a resigned nod. "Thought it was a wiener, I s'pose."

Now that you mention it, said the dog, it did bear a striking resemblance.

"So," concluded Homer, his voice as matter-of-fact as it'd been all along, "that puts the finish to 'er." He reached out and patted the dog in an absentminded way.

"Dogs do love a wiener," said Gummersong.

We do, said the dog. We thrive on them.

The publishing party for the bear's book was held in a downtown warehouse that'd been gutted to house the newest, hottest disco. The walls were brick with exposed electrical conduits. Brick pillars supported the cavernous interior; catwalks on four sides formed balconies; posters of James Dean and Marilyn Monroe hung behind the bar, while living legends moved about on the crowded floor. The bear's frowning face with its suspicious, beady eyes was on the latest *GQ*. There'd been interviews in *Publishers Weekly* and *The Village Voice*. Advance raves were already in from several magazines, along with enthusiastic quotes from distinguished writers welcoming Hal Jam into the inner circle.

The bear had personally chosen the food for the party. The buffet table was covered with pies and cakes. Other refreshments included pitchers of honey and maple syrup. On every table were Michel Guerard's slender chocolate leaves and Gaston Le Notre's delicate French caramels, selected by the bear from Bloomingdale's Au Chocolat Shop. He'd also insisted on bringing his Venus lamp, which stood among the pies and cakes like a strange fetish.

Bettina sped about in the crowd, spilling drinks and arranging photo opportunities. She clapped Boykins on the back. "We're slam-dunking tonight, Chum. We've got shots of Hal with Dr. Ruth and Henry Kissinger, and who else matters in this world?"

Professor Kenneth Penrod of Columbia talked about the decline of literature, and his rival, Samuel Ramsbotham of NYU, talked about the decline of Kenneth Penrod. "Penrod places too much emphasis on the writer," said Ramsbotham. "Any real study of contemporary literature begins with those who teach it. The teacher is the key, for it's the teacher who creates that all-important entity, the reader. It's not that I consider *myself* of any importance. I don't mind admitting I've learned most of what I know from my students. It's a radical view, but what are the students saying? What are they reading?" Professor Ramsbotham's students were reading what he made them read and first on the list were the anthologies he'd edited, for which he received a royalty check every six months. "What I think I've detected," he said sotto voce to the bear, "is a new kind of reader. Simple in his taste. Bored with conventional narrative and looking for work with strong visual content. I think we're going to see an end to the traditional novel, with all its self-referential mania. What do you think?"

"Whipped cream," said the bear, ladling a healthy portion onto a slice of pecan pie.

"My point exactly," said Ramsbotham. "Why take basic human experience and churn it up into something else? Very nicely put, Jam."

The music throbbed, and the bear nodded happily whenever anyone picked up a sweet. My party, he said to himself proudly. Going off without a hitch. He held a caramel up to the light. Everything a piece of candy should be. He popped it into his mouth, and the tips of his fangs gleamed. Most bears couldn't handle an evening like this. They'd probably tense up and bite someone.

His guests found him an unusually modest host, more concerned with their enjoyment than his own. "He doesn't play the Great Writer at all," remarked a young woman from *Women's Wear Daily*.

"All these pastries are suicidal," said a young woman from *Esquire*. "I just had two thousand calories in one bite." They were standing with the gold-tinted plaster Venus between them, unashamedly overweight, beads of illuminated oil dripping down around her voluptuous hips.

"I think he's trying to tell us to drop our ideal of the starved body."

"For that alone, he should get the National Book Award." The young woman from *Esquire* took a piece of chocolate cake.

"I hear he's *involved,*" said the woman from *Women's Wear Daily,* nodding toward Eunice Cotton.

"But is he *really* involved with her? I heard they were just friends."

"I suppose it's hard to tell. I mean, *she's* such a weirdo."

"We should be so weird."

"Well, that's true. Four best-sellers in a row. I can't read them myself."

"Oh, I don't know, *Angels in Bed* was amusing."

"Did you think so? I thought it was like having sex with a heating pad."

The bear came by, pleased to see females eating chocolate cake. Human females, in his observation, didn't take advantage of the wonderful range of sweets available to them. He turned, responding to a light tap on his shoulder, and saw a slender young woman in large eyeglasses holding a microphone toward him.

"Carmen DaCosta, WFMU. What writer has influenced you the most?"

The bear shuffled uncomfortably for a moment, paw in his mouth, then pointed to the only writer he knew—Eunice Cotton.

"Eunice?" she asked, turning off the microphone. "That's kind of odd, coming from a literary heavyweight. I like Eunice's books, they're fun, but do you take them seriously?"

"Pastry," said the bear, trying to return the conversation to the essentials.

"That's what I always felt. But you're implying they're more than that?"

"More sweets." He struggled to clarify. "Sweets are good."

Carmen pushed her glasses up onto her nose with her middle finger. She had a quick mind, made even quicker by the high levels of sugar now in her bloodstream. "I think I see what you mean. Eunice's sweet pop angels are a balance for the bitterness of the nineties?"

The bear nodded, his mouth stuffed with marzipan. I'm fielding questions well today, he said to himself.

"And you don't mind admitting you can learn from pop philosophy? That's very refreshing, Mr. Jam. I hate literary snobbery myself. I mean, why should I feel guilty if I read a book of Eunice's and it gives me a nice gooey feeling? So what if she pushes all my buttons? It's healthy. Tell you what, can we get together for a longer interview? When it's quieter?"

Bettina stepped in. "I bet Hal hasn't told you how much he admires your show, Carmen. Shall we set up an in-depth interview for tomorrow?"

The two women walked off together and the bear gave a small sigh of relief. When humans talked to him, his mind seemed to skid to a halt. I'm still a little insecure, he said to himself. With time, it will pass. He imagined himself chattering brightly to people, making all the quick human sounds of conversation. Bound to be a break-through soon, he told himself. I've only growled a few times all evening.

"Are you writing a new book?" asked a voice at his elbow.

The bear shook his head. "I can't find one."

"It'll happen," said Alice Dillby, a young editorial assistant at Cavendish Press. She wanted very much to be helpful, and her enthusiasm was fueled by the excitement of the party and the honey circulating in her system. "What do you think your problem is?"

"I've looked under every tree."

"But you have something you'd like to write about, don't you?"

"No," said the bear.

Alice gazed at him with admiration. What she loved best in a man, and seldom found, was modesty. That was why Hal Jam had such tremendous presence, because he carried himself without pretense. "You've really lived," she said.

"In a cave." He sipped at his honey, undisturbed by his confession, as he now knew that people always heard things differently from the way he meant them. He found it strange that he was the cause of this huge celebration, he a bear. I made all this happen, he said to himself, because I was in the right place at the right time. Opportunity came along in a briefcase and I grabbed it. I've never looked back.

She sensed he was trying to teach her something important. "A cave?"

"In winter."

"You're talking about Plato? His myth of the cave?"

"Cozy cave. You dream."

"Yes, yes," assented Alice ecstatically. "We accept the dream in the cave instead of our real, true self. Who of us really lives out our ideal?"

Alice's voice began to blend with the other voices at the party. The deep spaces of the disco buzzed, and the bear's ears rotated forward, as if toward impending danger. The current of his happiness switched to fear. Lights flashed on Alice's skin, turning it neon white and red, causing her somewhat toothy face to pulse aggressively.

". . . like to take your photo with the mayor, Mr. Jam, please . . ." He was jerked away from Alice, and a flash went off. The buzzing grew louder and the space that held it deepened in a terrifying way . . . humanity . . . humanity . . . a bear's only enemy.

"Hal, I'd like you to meet . . . from *Psychology Today* . . ."

". . . the way your heroine learns to advocate for herself . . ."

The sinister space continued to enlarge, with grotesque human forms emerging out of it, jabbering, gesticu-

151

lating, threatening. He pushed his way across the disco floor. Gadson grabbed him. "Hal, we did it." Gadson's arm came drunkenly around the bear's shoulder. "We showed them time-honored American copulation and they loved it. Now let's mix in something more exotic. Let's challenge their sexual stereotypes. Let's *Begin the Beguine*."

The bear evaded Gadson's grip and continued toward the door. Professor Penrod stepped in front of him. "The fish symbolism in your book . . . the fishing pole . . ."

The bear darted around the influential professor and rushed toward the entrance of the disco, heedless of the curious stares of the guests at his party.

"Well!" exclaimed the editor from *Women's Wear Daily* as she watched him go out through the door. "I think it's refreshing. I mean, authors *play* at being publicity shy, but did you ever see . . . ?"

"What's he doing to us?" cried Gadson to Bettina. "Doesn't he know how much this goddamned party is costing?"

Eunice also saw the bear's retreat and hurried after him. At her first publishing party, before her personal transition from hairdresser to author was complete, she'd freaked out too, suspicious that people were making fun of her when they praised her angels. "Hal, wait!"

The bear was hurrying away down the street, paws over his ears, trying to block out the sounds of the human world. He sniffed the air, hoping to find that scent he used to follow in the forest, which drew him toward a sunlit slope where wild irises bloomed. From there he'd been able to look into an enchanting valley that held all the things a bear cared most about—fish, nuts, berries, and the soft silence of the day in which to gather them. The company of crows was enough, their wing beats fanning the still air, their piercing cry bringing him news of the owl, the eagle, the hawk. The foxes withdrew as he approached. He was king in that valley. As the acrid fumes of Manhattan filled his nose, he felt his great heart breaking. He'd thrown paradise away, for fame and honey.

"Hal, please, wait for me!" Eunice raced after him, hair streaming, perfume trailing, high heels clicking. "Hal, please!" She caught up with him, grabbed him by the sleeve. He turned with a roar and she was struck to the heart by his unhappiness. "My poor darling," she cried, and threw her arms around him, indifferent to the two photographers who'd followed her down the street, led by Bettina, who was yelling at them to grab this photo opportunity of her top writers having a lovers' quarrel.

Flashes were popping, and the automatic winders of the cameras were whirring, as Bettina's lust for good photo coverage raised her voice to a shriek. "Be sure you get cleavage!"

Eunice spun toward her. "Bettina, how could you?" After which she graciously obliged the photographers with a profound glimpse of cleavage, then threw her arms back around the bear. "I understand how you feel, Hal. I've been through it all myself." She stroked his face as her visionary eyes filled with tears. "The cheap and tawdry ritual of success. It's monstrous, it's wounding. But it's the price we have to pay for being rich and famous. And my angels have assured me it's all right to be rich and famous. The angels *like* rich and famous."

Arthur Bramhall and Vinal Pinette slid down a wooded ravine at twilight to the mouth of a cave. Bramhall sniffed the opening thoroughly and cautiously. The smell was of pine boughs and bear. He crept in, over the dried needles that covered the floor.

"How's she look?" asked Pinette, appearing behind him at the doorway of the cave, into which the twilight streamed.

"Abandoned."

Pinette crept into the cave and squatted down on the dried boughs. "Uncle Filbert tried cave life once. Leonora Spraggins was after him, as he'd put a bun in her oven, and Leonora's five brothers was after him too."

Bramhall squatted down with his back against the wall. The whirl of the world was far away. There was only the smell of bear and pine boughs and the view through the cave door to the trees. A sigh of comfort went through him, as of some larger creature whose requirements were not easily met, and for whom a spacious cave such as this was just the ticket.

"To complicate matters for Filbert the

police was on him too, for rigging a bingo game. So a nice cave was just the ticket."

Bramhall crawled outside to a nearby pine, snapped off enough boughs to fill his arms, and returned. Pinette watched him lay the boughs down. "Filbert come out to a bright new future. The police had forgot about him and Leonora had found herself another suitor who fit the bill even though he did have a goiter on the back of his neck the size of a seed potato. You think we should write this down? My memory ain't what it used to be and we might never catch hold of this material again. I believe it's the stuff of pop'lar entertainment."

Bramhall sat on the fresh boughs, feeling more secure in this cave shaped a million years ago than he'd felt even in his barn or in Gummersong's hut. The enclosure had sheltered countless generations of animals, and he felt their affection for it, as if the walls of the cave held memories of their feeling.

"Uncle Filbert must have done some deep thinking during his spell of denning, because a little while after he come out he wangled himself a loan from the government and started up his own grocery business. He'd have been a rich man today if he hadn't made one little mistake." Pinette gazed through the somber light of the cave toward Bramhall.

"What was Uncle Filbert's mistake?" asked Bramhall.

"He used to drink himself to sleep every night with a

jug of wine, which in itself don't entail much risk. But one night he reached for his jug and fetched up a jug of Clorox instead. We found him next morning stiffer'n a rolling pin, finger hooked in the empty Clorox jug." Pinette nodded his head solemnly in the shadows. "So right there we got ourselves an instructive tale about what and what not to keep by the bedside. That kind of story has an audience."

Bramhall saw, caught in the jagged face of the cave wall, strands of coarse fur left by the previous occupant. He felt the comings and goings of this creature as it huffed in and out of the lodging, doing as he'd just done, making a comfortable bed for itself. He felt its bulk, its awesome power, its imperial claim to this space. And he knew, with a strange inner certainty, that it would not be returning.

"Hal, this is Bettina. It's time for you to go to your interview. Remember? You're taping with Bryant Gumbel. A limo will be waiting for you outside your building. I'll meet you at NBC." Bettina was in her office at Cavendish Press, talking on her headset telephone, which left both her hands free to deal with the paperwork generated by Hal Jam's tour. Four-color brochures had gone out to every important newspaper, television and radio station in the country, and doors had opened. Within the folder was an excerpt from the novel which *The New Yorker* had run, and a fascinating bio of Jam invented by Bettina. There were a number of witty remarks of Jam's, also invented by Bettina. A five-by-seven glossy photo had been included, of the bear, strikingly lit and looking seriously literary.

Bettina hung up and looked at her assistant. "I don't think he realizes how hard it is to get on the *Today* show. I do hope he and Bryant Gumbel will get along."

· · ·

The bear descended the elevator in his apartment building, greeted the doorman politely, stepped outside, caught a whiff of Central Park, and walked directly on by the waiting limo, which was driven by Zinatoon Nipunik, of Lightning Limo. Nipunik was stooping to retrieve a fallen ball of falafel which had squirted from his pita bread onto the floor of the limo, and so he missed his passenger's approach.

The bear plunged into the park. It was the first winter he'd spent awake, and he savored the solemn landscape. That great time-waster, hibernation, in which he'd lost years of his life, was unneeded now that he had central heating. He rolled in the dry grass, kicked his paws at the sky, and emitted a soft, pleasure-filled growl. Then he felt a troubling shadow cross his mind, about something he was supposed to do. What, what, what?

Interview!

Where?

Somewhere.

Somewhere, somewhere, somewhere.

With somebody.

Who?

Don't tell me, wait, I know it.

His tongue ran over his snout as it came to him. Gumball!

He came up out of the park onto Central Park West,

and knew he had everything under control as soon as he saw the subway entrance.

He was fond of subway entrances because of their cavelike appearance. He rarely passed a subway entrance without descending into it. Then, once he was down below, the echoing tunnels made him feel at home. On one of these descents he'd discovered gumballs, which were dispensed from round glass globes attached to posts on the subway platform. Had his cave in the forest had a gumball dispensing machine he might never have felt the desire to leave. But again, it had been up to mankind, with its superior mental powers, to make this great stride forward.

He descended now, into the subway, through the turnstile, and onto the platform. Sure enough, there was a gumball machine.

I'm doing beautifully here, he said to himself as he approached the machine.

He inserted a quarter in its slot, turned the crank, and out rolled a large red gumball. He took it in his paw and gazed at it.

Interview.

With a gumball.

He waited, and while subway trains came and went and the gumball sat unmoving in his paw, he wondered if perhaps there was something he'd missed.

He popped the gumball into his mouth.

The vivid red dye which coated the gumball melted

onto his tongue, and the carcinogens within flowed over his taste buds, absolutely first-rate.

He chewed happily, feeling that, after all, the mission had turned out well. He was interviewing a gumball. Publicity was easy. He wondered why the little birdlike female at his publisher's was so worried about it all the time.

A subway train rattled into the station. He got on it. It was the first time he'd been on a train, but today was a day for breaking new ground.

He sat down and the car started. He stared at the subway tunnel walls rushing past; he chewed his gumball thoughtfully.

He rode along through a great many stops, until he grew hungry. Time to get off, he said to himself, stood, and waited for the train to enter the next station. He surfaced in a neighborhood he'd never seen before. He walked along, sniffing the air, but before he'd gotten a complete sampling, a dominant male in a shiny red suit with big shoulders stopped him. The dominant male had two females with him, in short skirts. "Hey, brothah," said the dominant male, "you like to subagitate with the sisters of mercy here?"

The females smiled at him, and one of them angled her body toward the bear so her hip stuck out, and said, "You wan' some of my cat meat, honey?"

The bear *was* hungry, and he was grateful to her for

offering to share her cat meat, but it was not a favorite food of his. "No thank you," he said. "Good-bye."

"He's not here!" screamed Bettina into her cellular phone as she paced wildly on the sidewalk in front of NBC. "I hired your company to pick up my writer and bring him here and he's not here!"

"My driver dere," said Manfaluti Kheyboom, the owner of Lightning Limo. "He was front of boolding."

"Well, where is he now?"

"Driving."

"Without my writer?"

"Your writer not appear."

"What do you mean, he not appear? He left the building."

"My driver ask. Nobody know nutting."

"Well, nutting is what you're going to get paid."

"My driver lost t'ree hours."

"And I lost my *writer!*"

"Not my fault, lady. Fault your writer."

"Fault your mother!" said Bettina, and ended the call with a violent jab of her finger on the cellular disconnect button. Manfaluti Kheyboom shook his head sadly and thought to himself, you come to America, you struggle to learn language, you hire good driver, and all you get is misunderstandink.

. . .

The bear didn't know he was in Harlem, but he knew it was different from his own neighborhood. There was music floating from the windows, and the people seemed in less of a hurry than in other parts of town. They congregated on street corners, while people in his neighborhood just rushed along the sidewalk and didn't even look at each other. He felt himself relaxing and decided he would move here.

He was in his gray tweed suit and baseball hat, with his elastic tie, and he wished he had a shiny red suit like the one worn by the dominant male.

He walked on, sniffing his way through the smells that came from the restaurants. Watching him were two heavily armed children. They were brothers and the bigger kids called them the Tinys—Tiny One and Tiny Two. Tiny One had an IQ of 200, and had been able to read a newspaper since he was in diapers. His ambition was to be a criminal and drive a white Lincoln with gold-leaf chrome.

Tiny Two had discovered the principle of base-10 arithmetic while goofing with the beads on his playpen. He'd worked his way through complicated mathematical procedures before he could speak, and now calculated sums in his head with astonishing speed. His ambition was to control sixty blocks of Harlem selling caviar crack, from which he'd make a thousand dollars a day. Tiny One and Tiny Two knew they were the smartest people in Harlem, but older gang members still kicked their asses a lot. So they were on the lookout for opportunities to impress the older members. And this big buster who'd just walked into the neighborhood might be that opportunity. He was big, and he looked bad. "Probably trying to cut himself a piece of territory," said Tiny One.

"We be the ones doing the cutting," said Tiny Two, touching the concealed barrel of his submachine gun.

The bear was strolling happily along, doing his latest imitation of a human being. He was copying the walking style of the dominant male in the red suit, a rhythmic swaying of trunk and pelvis, and footsteps that rocked along the ground, as if testing it for solidity.

"Dude walking like a pimp," said Tiny One.

"He dressed awful square fo' a pimp."

The bear noticed some unusual hand gestures young people in this part of town made to each other when they met on the street, and he copied these too.

"Goddamn, he signing!" cried Tiny One. If anyone who wasn't a member of the ruling gang made hand signs, they had to die. "Putting the neighborhood down bad! Disrespecting the sign! I'm gonna pop the mothahfuckah!"

"We ain't in close enuf. Keep yo' cool."

Tiny One and Tiny Two moved along quickly. "I'm

gonna spray that big buster's ass *good* for signing like that," said Tiny One. Somewhere in his smart little self, he knew he was lost in a house of mirrors, but as he was only eight all he could think to do was grow bigger in the mirror.

"Yeah, he gonna sign fo' the last time today," said Tiny Two, who had a similarly vague awareness about himself. Sometimes his lightning math calculations arrived with thoughts about his future that frightened him, but they came and went too fast.

The Tinys drew closer to the bear. He'd stopped to listen to three males singing on a street corner. They sang the most beautiful music he'd ever heard. Their voices were locked in harmony, and his ears rotated with the loveliness of it. It sounded like this:

"Shooo-doop-en shooo-beee-doooo . . ."

Their close vocal harmony created a sound the bear felt he could touch with his paw.

"Fuckah be signing *again*," said Tiny Two.

"We got to get around the other side, or we liable to shoot the King Tones in the ass."

"Be great to take him down right 'longside the King Tones though."

"Yeah, they 'preciate a dramatic touch like that while they singing."

The King Tones were known individually as King Cobra, Kaiser Wilhelm, and Imperial Decree. Imperial Decree had been ingesting a new brand of paint thinner,

165

which gave his throat a coating he liked for singing. He had the deepest human voice the bear had ever heard, and the sweetest, like a heavy golden syrup pouring into the air from his throat. But Imperial Decree's eyes had begun to revolve in his head from the effects of paint thinner, and his knees were buckling.

"You okay, Imp?" asked King Cobra, the leader of the group.

"Be fine . . ." said the crumpled singer. "Jus' need to take a moment here . . ." Imperial Decree pressed his cheek against the pavement, as his head seemed to be rotating at an increasing rate of speed. "Got to . . . *stabilize* . . ."

"You sing from down there?"

"Sing anywhere."

"Okay, le's take it from the top again."

Tiny Two and Tiny One had realigned themselves so they had the proper trajectory on the Big Buster. "Now," said Tiny Two, "le's get down for the 'hood," and reached inside his shirt for his weapon.

"*Shooo-doooop-en shooooo be-doooooo . . .*"

The harmony floated out again, but the bear noted that a portion of it was missing. The singer with the deep voice was moving his lips but no music was coming out, only soft sputtering sounds.

"Shit, he out of it totally now," said King Cobra. "Vinyl resins fuck him up bad."

The bear opened his mouth, and suddenly a deep musical growl was coming out, for bears are tuneful beasts at heart. His tremendous barrel tone filled the air. The King Tones looked at him in surprise and resumed their singing, their eyes saying, *take it*.

The bear took it, floating happily in the song, becoming part of the dimension of harmony. His musical growl fit the pulsing bass line, and he poured all of his heart into it, his mighty diaphragm expanding and his breath resonating in his huge chest and stomach cavity.

Dude got a voice like the horn on the Staten Island ferry, observed King Cobra.

"We cain't kill him while he's singing," said Tiny One, pressing down the barrel of Tiny Two's gun. "The King Tones might think we disrespecting them."

"We wait till they's done," said Tiny Two.

The bear swayed to the tune as he sang, his eyes slitted in concentration, his voice rumbling along at the bottom of the vocal register. Kaiser Wilhelm sang in a strong falsetto, like a hawk on the wind, the sound piercingly sweet and sad, a sound the bear knew well and to which he blended his own thunderous rumbling. When the last note was reached, the leader threw his arm around the bear's shoulder and said, "Brothah, you sing yo' ass off."

Brother, thought the bear excitedly. His imitation

of a human must have been perfect. What a break-through!

"Okay," said Tiny Two, "song's over, we kin pop him now."

As Two and One drew their guns, King Cobra looked their way. "What the fuck you think you doing?"

"That big buster was signin'," said Tiny Two. "He was disrespectin' the 'hood."

"Get the fuck outa here fo' I kick yo' fucking ass," said King Cobra, who was himself only five feet three but commanded great respect in the neighborhood for his musical abilities. "This be ouh soul brothah." He tightened his grip around the bear's shoulder. "Man got a sound like he got, I don' give a fuck what he signs. You understand me?"

"Yessir," said the two Tinys as they put away their weapons.

"Go beat yo' tiny baloney 'stead of messing around where you ain't wanted."

The two Tinys slunk back, and King Cobra said to the bear, "Crazy little mothahfuckahs got nothing better to do than shoot peoples up. They don't know they's a time and place fo' everythang. Now—let's do us a little rap."

The diminutive leader of the King Tones could rhyme eighty thousand words in single, double, and triple rhyme. The pulsing rhythm of his rap got the bear hopping up and down excitedly, his arms pistoning back and forth as he sang a drumlike bass-grunt accompaniment. Imperial Decree rolled onto his back and stared at the sky, the whites of his eyes the color of turpentine. He snapped his fingers weakly to the music. "Sound good," he said. "Sound *real* good."

After the tune was finished, King Cobra said to the bear, "It's time we got some food into the brother down there, to cut the effect of what he been ingesting. You up for a little bite to eat?"

"Subagitate with cat meat," said the bear, his left arm still pistoning to the beat.

King Cobra bent over Imperial Decree. "You able to rise and walk, Imp?"

"Think . . . I bes' stay put," said Imperial Decree, his bass voice resonating near the curb and his eyes pointing in different directions.

"Shit," said King Cobra, "bus liable to run over his ass, we leave him here."

The bear reached down and picked Imperial Decree up with one hand and laid him gently over his shoulder.

"Much . . . oblige," said Imperial Decree, hanging head-down.

"You got to give up paint thinner, my man, fo' it kill you," said King Cobra.

"Amen," moaned Imperial Decree.

Trailing behind the King Tones and the bear were

Tiny One and Tiny Two, hands on their concealed weapons. If the Big Buster caused any problems for the King Tones, they'd ventilate his ass.

"We got us a great restaurant up ahead, name of Ralph's," said King Cobra to the bear. "Every Tuesday afternoon Ralph got a seventy-five-cent special."

The bear nodded, his nose twitching with the smell that was coming from the restaurant fan. He was feeling very good about the way this day was going. He'd interviewed a gumball, and now he'd made friends, one of whom was hanging over his shoulder.

They entered the small restaurant, which was crowded with people from the neighborhood. It had a few tables with plastic flowers on them; a counter with several wobbly stools faced the window. The bear sniffed the air and liked what he smelled. He removed his new friend from his shoulder and propped him up by the window.

King Cobra read from a blackboard on which the seventy-five-cent Tuesday special was advertised. "Fried chicken, french fries, salad, and two slices of bread. Best deal in town." He leaned toward the bear and said quietly, "Ralph bankrupting himself with the seventy-five-cent special. But he got to see folks eating."

The bear nodded. He understood. When you saw people eating, generally they weren't eating you.

Ralph appeared in the serving window, sending through a special. He was not directly aware that he was bankrupting himself with his special. He knew something wasn't adding up, but it didn't occur to him to question his seventy-five-cent special, because when folks came in, sat down, and ate a good meal of chicken fried in his special batter, he felt everything come together for him. He looked over at Imperial Decree, propped up in the corner. Into the turpentine again, I s'pose. Sing like Pavarotski too. "You oughta make a record," called out Ralph to Imperial Decree.

"It's hard to break in," replied King Cobra.

"I broke in," said the bear.

"That a fac'?"

"Through the back window."

"Different kind of break I'm referring to," said King Cobra. He was starting to realize that the Big Buster had a glitch in the head. One of them big slow dudes never caught up to the rest of the class. "We're trying to get into show business, you know what I'm saying? But we ain't made the right connection."

"Publicity," said the bear.

"Come again?"

"They do have a fabulous sound," said Bettina.

Bettina lived in alphabet city on the Lower East Side, on a grungy street that was not particularly safe, but she owned an entire house there, two floors of which she occupied herself. The street was made safer today by Tiny One and Tiny Two guarding her door. The Tinys had whined their way into being allowed to come along. King Cobra had finally relented, as there were people in this neighborhood who wanted to kill him for business reasons, and the Tinys were lethal protectors.

The bear sat with a plate of food on his lap, concentrating on it. He was pleased with himself for having brought Bettina and the King Tones together. He'd called her and she'd sent a limo immediately, and they'd all ridden in it, eating olives and peanuts.

". . . 'preciate you bringing us, bro'," said King Cobra softly, beside him on the couch. "Kind of exposure we been needing."

"No problem," said the bear.

"You evah need somebody bopped," said the little rapper, "you call the King Tones, we be there for you."

The buzzer door on the apartment sounded and the Tinys opened the door for Chum Boykins.

Boykins looked down in astonishment at two little boys holding mini-machine guns in their hands.

"You here fo' Miz Quint?" demanded Tiny One.

"He's all right," called Bettina from the living room.

"All right?" exclaimed Boykins as he strode into the living room. "What's going on here, Bettina?"

"Chum, meet the King Tones."

"How do you do?" said Boykins, nodding to the members of the group.

"Doing jus' fine," said King Cobra, "owing to the kindness of some good, good people." King Cobra smiled toward Bettina and the Big Buster. He now knew that the Big Buster did not have a glitch in the head but was actually a famous writer, ready to share his contacts with a brother. The knowledge of who the Big Buster and his friends were had also changed the feelings of the Tinys. When they walked into Bettina's apartment, the first thing they saw was the life-size point-of-purchase cardboard image of the seven-foot-two basketball great Fahmahoo Shameel, who'd written a best-selling autobiography for Cavendish Press. The Tinys stared wide-eyed at the life-size Shameel, and Bettina said they could have it, thereby sealing their feelings toward her. They silently swore an oath of loyalty to her and caused their machine pistols to make clicking sounds of readiness. Now they sat side by side on Bettina's couch and helped themselves to Bettina's homemade poppyseed cake.

Bettina looked at Boykins. "Want to hear more good news?" she asked. "Hal missed his interview with Bryant Gumbel today."

"Gumball," said the bear, nodding affirmatively.

"Oh god no," said Boykins. "Did you patch it up?"

"Bryant was very understanding," said Bettina. "We go back a long way."

"You must never let Hal out of your sight," said Boykins.

"We watch him fo' you!" said Tiny One. "Make sure he get where he got to go."

"Bettina, we're responsible for Hal as if he were our child," said Boykins. "He's not used to cities. They confuse him."

"It won't happen again, Chum. Now just listen to the music."

"I must say I'm deeply concerned at being met at your door by armed children."

"Chum, who do you know in the music business?"

"I know people. Why?"

"Because the King Tones are going to be big, and you could be part of it."

"I'm a literary agent, Bettina."

"I'm talking megahit time, Chum."

"I see." Boykins was up to a forty megahit dose of Prozac, his serotonin level was high, and Mickey Mouse's harsh demands for obeisance had all but faded. The King Tones looked as if they would present major worries, as one of them had wing nuts in his hair and another smelled strongly of turpentine. He had to ask himself, will another problem client neutralize the wonders of Prozac and turn me back into an automaton?

"King Cobra, Kaiser Wilhelm, and Imperial Decree," said Bettina.

"King Cobra . . . Kaiser Wilhelm . . . and Imperial Decree . . ." Boykins had opened his notebook and was writing in his small, precise hand. Then he looked at the children on Bettina's couch. "And who are they?"

"We the Tinys," said Tiny One, his cheeks stuffed with cake.

"They're going to be regular visitors," said Bettina, who had fallen for the Tinys. Their angry little faces, their paranoid little gazes, and their brilliant little brains had stolen her little heart. She looked at the Tinys now and was suffused with henlike feelings for them. They were a pair of prodigies, wandering in a cloud.

The King Tones began to sing, and the bear looked on with great pleasure. People were eating cake and his new friends now had what every human being needed, an agent and a publicist.

Vinal Pinette walked through the woods alone, through swirling snow. When he came to the steep hillside he worked his way slowly down it to the cave.

The day was bright and the air still; a blue jay fluttered by, piercing the air with its sharp cry and then sailing on down the valley. Pinette pushed aside the pine boughs that covered the mouth of the cave and crawled in.

Arthur Bramhall was far back in the darkness, curled up on a bed of grass and pine boughs. The wall of the cave was spotted with frost. Pinette watched Bramhall breathing and marveled at the depth of his sleep. "I knowed you was tough, Art, and here's the proof of it."

Pinette squatted on his haunches, keeping his friend company.

"Is he in there?" asked a voice from behind him.

He turned and saw the fur-bearing woman standing outside the entrance.

"Yup," he said, backing out through the cave door.

"You don't think that he'll freeze to death?"

"He's got a rhythm going. You break it, he could croak. Leastwise, that's my view of it." Pinette shook the snow off the peak of his cap and readjusted it. "They say that an Eskimo can just curl up in his igloo and doze for months. Some make it, some don't."

The fur-bearing woman had great respect for Vinal Pinette, whom she saw as an elder who knew the ways of the forest. "He's on a spirit quest, isn't he?"

"Whatever he's on, I ain't one to interfere. Not when a man's got a rhythm."

Pinette and the fur-bearing woman walked back through the woods together, along a path the snow was rapidly covering.

The bear's appearances on the network morning shows weren't easy for him. He did not fully grasp what a television studio was, and each visit to one filled him with anxiousness. But Bryant Gumbel had been impressed: Hal Jam had not once mentioned the title of his book during their interview. Gumbel felt this was the mark of a real artist, who didn't feel the need to point to his work; actually the bear had forgotten what the title was. When Harry Smith interviewed him on CBS *This Morning*, Bettina had the title written on the bear's shirt cuff, which he looked at throughout the entire interview, but referred to the book as *Shirt Cuff*. With some trepidation, Bettina put him on the air shuttle to Boston.

I'm the first bear in the air, he said to himself as he looked at the earth far below him. Seat's a little snug, but they give you peanuts. Everything a bear needs to tide him over.

When he entered the Boston terminal he was met by a plump woman holding up a copy of his book. "Hi, I'm Julie Moody, your media escort." The bear followed her dutifully. Just my type of female. The bearish silhouette. Smells about forty-two.

After they claimed his luggage, she led him out of the terminal into the parking lot. "I'll have to take you straight to your first interview. After that you get a break and can settle into your hotel. Here's my car."

She opened the front door and he climbed in.

"I love your book," said Mrs. Moody as she got behind the wheel. "It's so romantic." She gave him a sideways glance. "Was it all imagination?"

"I found it under a tree."

"Where lightning strikes," agreed Mrs. Moody as she worked her way through the heavy terminal traffic. "Dear me, what a mess, and you've got a live interview. Do you think we might fit through there?" She took her car off the road, into a restricted airport construction site, past large pieces of earthmoving equipment and construction workers hysterically waving flags and shouting at her. She waved back and drove on through the site, then back out onto the road, far ahead of the traffic jam. She stole another glance at her novelist. "You write so beautifully about nature," she said with a sigh. She was now speeding along the highway toward Boston. As she worked the brake and accelerator with dexterity, her skirt rose above her knees. Remarkable the variety of shape you get in the human female leg, thought the bear to himself. Lady bears all have pretty much the same fuzzy shape.

He closed his eyes and breathed Mrs. Moody's numerous provocative scents, concentrated within the confined space of her car. Mrs. Moody got the strangest feeling, as if she were riding naked. *Gracious*, she thought to herself, and rolled her window down.

They entered Boston and threaded their way through city traffic toward the TV studio. The bear rode quietly and comfortably, looking curiously at people, and at Mrs. Moody's legs, admiring them. There were no thoughts in his head. He enjoyed looking at the people and at Mrs. Moody's legs. Streets came and went, and Mrs. Moody's legs moved as she drove, and his mind was like a tranquil lake, in which passing images were reflected.

"You're very quiet," said Mrs. Moody. "Do you like to meditate before you give an interview?"

"What's an interview?"

"It's good to be a little blasé. But you don't want to lose your spontaneity. I've seen it happen to so many authors. After a few dozen interviews, they start giving the same answers to the same questions, and all their freshness is gone."

The bear had no idea what she was talking about, so he looked out the window. He sensed that human understanding was something like a net, with loops being added to it constantly, and he could imagine a human being nimbly casting this net; but when he imagined this net of understanding in his own paws he saw himself getting

180

tangled in it, and finally being brought to his knees, piti-fully thrashing about inside the shimmering mesh as shad-owy figures approached with clubs.

Mrs. Moody pulled into a parking lot. The bear climbed out and followed her into a large building. A security guard issued them identity cards. The bear smoothed his out carefully as they walked along. "Hal Jam," he said, looking down at the letters that spelled his name. He liked having this identity card because it showed everyone he had an identity.

"We go in here," said Mrs. Moody, "to the green room."

"It's not green," remarked the bear as they sat down in the small waiting area.

"Green rooms usually aren't," said Mrs. Moody.

Again, he marveled at the complexity of human be-ings, who called a room green when it wasn't green. What did it mean?

A young man entered the green room that wasn't green and said, "You're Hal Jam?"

The bear pointed to the identity card on his lapel. The young man put out his hand. "I'm Scott Emery, assis-tant producer. We'll be going on in about five minutes. Can I get you anything?"

"Popcorn," said the bear, who often confused be-ing on TV with watching TV. This was because he was a bear.

"I don't think we have any," said Scott Emery. "We have some Cheesy Things, though."

"Good," said the bear.

Scott Emery went away and returned a few moments later with Cheesy Things in a bag. "I hope these'll take the edge off. I'll be back when we're ready for you." He switched on a monitor mounted on the green-room wall, which carried the interview now in progress—a doctor discussing the latest surgical techniques.

The bear nibbled the Cheesy Things contentedly, and Mrs. Moody was impressed by his calm manner. Authors got very little actual airtime, and their publicists had told them that every word counted and that they must speak in sound bites. Consequently, young authors especially were filled with nervous tension beforehand, as they tried to rehearse their sound bites. But the only bites Hal Jam seemed to be concerned about were those he was taking out of his Cheesy Things.

Scott Emery returned and announced they were ready for him. The bear followed Emery onto a set built around a working fireplace. The anchor woman was in one of the chairs beside the fireplace. *Destiny and Desire* was in front of her on a low table, and the book was glowing.

"Hal," said Scott Emery, "if you'd just sit in this chair facing Sandy . . ."

The bear sat down and Sandy Kincaid smiled at him.

"I genuinely liked your book," she said. "We'll say good things about it."

"I'm Hal Jam," he said, and pointed to his name card.

"Yes," said Scott Emery, "let's get rid of that, shall we, and replace it with a microphone."

A sound technician clipped the microphone onto the bear's lapel and returned to his console. "Could you say something, please?"

The bear said, "Up your ass," and the technician chuckled. "Fine, I've got a level."

Scott Emery said, "When we go on, speak directly toward Sandy."

The lights were switched on, bathing the bear and the anchor woman in bright light. On the adjacent set, the surgeon was just finishing his interview, which was audible now, over the studio speakers. ". . . like to finish by saying that with laser surgery, removing the gall bladder is a very simple matter . . ."

Removing the gall bladder? The bear stared into the blinding lights. The dark space beyond them seemed to grow, as if he were in a gigantic cavern controlled by creatures with dangerously burning eyes.

"One minute to go," said a voice from the darkness.

The bear rose in his seat. He'd been tricked! They were going to remove his gall bladder and put it in a bottle!

"Please, Hal," said Scott Emery, "we only have thirty seconds . . ."

The bear let out a roar and the sound man clutched his earphones in pain as his vu-meter leapt into the red zone. Scott Emery hissed to his cameramen to stand by. If his crew handled a live nervous breakdown with taste and dignity, Scott Emery, young producer, would get a nice red apple from the station manager. "I've got it," said the man on camera one, swinging quickly to cover the guest's erratic movement, which now included lifting Scott Emery into the air and shaking him.

"Twenty seconds . . ."

Sandy Kincaid watched in fascination. A best-selling author assaulting an assistant producer on the air could help her faltering ratings. People complained that she was too sweet. Well, she'd show them. She put on her most serious-face-of-journalism and prepared to deliver the hard edge of the morning to Boston, as the bear tossed Scott Emery onto an off-camera prop table, amidst a display of the latest in computerized kitchen aids.

Mrs. Moody charged across the set, came in behind Jam, and stroked him gently behind the ears. "Hal, it's Julie," she said softly. "Here are your Cheesy Things."

She'd raised five children and taken twelve hundred authors around, and she hadn't lost one yet. Her hands slipped down to his massive shoulders, caressing them. "It's all right, Hal. Just sit down, and eat your Cheesy

Things. This nice woman only wants to ask you a few questions and then I'll take you back to the hotel."

"Five, four, three . . ."

The bear sat back down.

"I'll be right here," said Mrs. Moody as she stepped out beyond the cameras. The bear stared into the menacing darkness. He sniffed, and Mrs. Moody's scent was still in the air. Its familiarity calmed him, as did his Cheesy Things. He turned toward the brightly lit young woman seated across from him and sniffed her.

"My guest today is Hal Jam, author of the best-selling novel *Destiny and Desire*, a book everybody seems to love, both critics and public alike. I've just finished it, and I found it wonderfully fresh, and yet somehow it manages to reaffirm some very important values. Hal, good morning."

"I'm Hal Jam."

"You certainly are," said Sandy Kincaid, smiling perkily while trying to psych this maniac out. She didn't want him attacking *her* on the air, no matter what it did for the ratings. "You obviously know the great outdoors— the fishing scenes are wonderful—but you also know women, Hal. How does someone who has lived so far from civilization have so much wisdom concerning the inner life of the opposite sex?"

The bear ate the last Cheesy Thing and then stuck his nose in the bag. Then he looked at the pretty young woman sitting across from him. He felt words bubbling inside him, as if Sandy Kincaid's swift chatty style was in him now. To his great surprise, chatty words bubbled swiftly out of him. "When I lived in the woods I only did it once a year."

Sandy Kincaid blinked, reddened, and pushed on. "The degree of tenderness you've created in this rural atmosphere is one of the things critics are raving about. It leads me to this question: Are you saying that tenderness is impossible in our hurried city life? Is sexual tenderness more likely to occur between two people in a quiet country setting?"

The bear stuck his long tongue into the Cheesy Things bag and licked up all the salt. "When I did it in the forest, if I wasn't careful I could get badly mauled."

Sandy Kincaid looked nervously past the bear toward Scott Emery, who, in spite of having been thrown among the computerized kitchen aids, was waving to her, encouraging her to run with the interview. The cameramen were smiling, and the rest of the studio staff, who were usually half-asleep, were all listening attentively.

The bear crossed his stumpy legs and turned the bag inside out to lick it more thoroughly. And more chatty words bubbled out of him. "I had to hold on really tight from behind or those females would have torn me apart."

Sandy Kincaid's eyes revealed a certain unsteadiness. "Are we talking about any particular female? I mean, was there a model for your heroine?"

"We're talking about a big bear female."

"Well, yes, I suppose she would be bare," laughed Sandy Kincaid nervously.

"Now that I live in the city, I do it more often, but it's safer."

Sandy Kincaid switched to her politically correct voice. "We're all committed to safe sex."

"A bear female in heat is touchy," explained the bear.

The director turned to his assistant. "What?"

"Hal," continued Sandy Kincaid, gamely pressing on, "you've become an overnight sensation. Have you changed because of it?"

"This morning," said the bear, quickly opening his suit jacket and pulling the edge of his underpants out over his belt.

Sandy Kincaid looked back down at the book and tried to bring order to her wildly racing thoughts. "If you could sum up your impressions of urban life in a single word or two—"

"Cheesy Things," said the bear, lifting the empty bag in the hope of getting more.

"Do you mean that urban values are cheesy because everything's been commercialized? But that's how a civilized society works. Isn't it slightly unfair of you to hold the mirror of rural life up to us and say, *you must live like this?* Modern city life is cheesy of necessity."

"You don't like Cheesy Things?"

"I'm not saying I don't *like* them. I'm saying those cheesy things *have* to exist." Sandy Kincaid felt herself on somewhat firmer ground now. She had strong political opinions, gathered from the wire service to which her station subscribed. "I'm saying we're stuck with them."

The bear squinted toward the lights. Talking so much had made him hungry. "I want more Cheesy Things."

"I understand your view, that we've become greedy consumerists," said Sandy Kincaid, hoping that the interview was finally getting a rhythm. "But we can't all just move back to the woods and be like the people in your book."

"It's my book," said the bear aggressively.

"Yes, certainly, and you have the right to do whatever you please in it, but can a work of fiction actually hope to change society's views?" Sandy Kincaid was hoping to relax a bit, now that they were safely lost in meaningless abstractions.

"Sex and pizza," said the bear.

"But, Hal, don't you think it's too easy to just write American culture off as hopelessly mired in 'sex and pizza,' as you call it?"

"Your legs really glow," remarked the bear, gazing down at the glossy sheen of her ankles, calves, and the bit of thigh showing beneath the studio lights.

"Leg shot," said the director from his control booth,

and as the camera tilted, added, "I like this yo-yo. Who is he?"

Sandy Kincaid, having lost the point she'd been trying to make, said, "I've been talking with Hal Jam. The name of the book is *Destiny and Desire*."

"I'm Hal Jam," said the bear.

Bettina, watching the show on satellite from her office in New York, turned to Elliot Gadson and said, "Tell me I'm crazy. But I think he's a natural."

"Natural is not quite the word I'd use to describe him," said Elliot Gadson. "But he certainly is memorable."

Following his interview, Mrs. Moody drove the bear to the Ritz Carlton. The car had hardly stopped when a top-hatted doorman with white gloves and the motions of a masterfully manipulated puppet opened the car door, and the bear ambled out.

"Good morning, sir," said the doorman, and gestured briskly toward the front door. "After you, please. I'll see to the luggage." Mrs. Moody led her author into the lobby to the reception desk. "This is Mr. Jam," she said to the young woman behind the desk.

The young woman gave the guest a welcoming smile. "You're in room 32, Mr. Jam, facing the park." She handed the room key to the bear. "Enjoy your stay."

Beside the reception desk, the concierge handled the requests that came from the hotel's guests. The bear was sniffing the lobby, and the concierge was sniffing him, figuratively speaking; the concierge could smell money, and his treatment of a guest was based on just how strong the scent was. A South American cattle baron, short, compact, bristling with authority, had a rich scent; the gaunt chairman of a merchant bank, tall, spectral, had a rich scent; the vice president of the United States, who was currently ensconced in the largest suite in the hotel, had a rich scent. This new gentleman he wasn't sure about, as he observed him from the corner of his eye. The gentleman's suit was a good one and fit him perfectly; his tie was decidedly a question mark. He had an authoritative presence, with his barrel chest and large head, but there was something strained about his posture, as if he were forcing it. The old rich were never strained, their ramrod posture steadied by the heads of those their forefathers had ground into the earth. Yet this burly gentleman did have an emanation of something very old about him. Studying him as he walked across the lobby toward the elevator, the concierge couldn't know that the bear's family was the oldest in America, having been there for 30 million years. The concierge decided it was best to rank him as *resembling* old money, until further clarification.

"Shall I come up and see that everything is okay?" asked Mrs. Moody. She stepped into the elevator with the bear, and the white-gloved elevator man closed the door. The perfume in the elevator was blended exclusively for the Ritz Carlton so that returning guests felt something like a familiar embrace when they rose toward their room once more. And for those new guests like Mr. Jam, it was a poignant little introduction to the hominess that awaited them. The bear sniffed appreciatively. They give you a key and tell you where to go. The elements of uncertainty, so troubling to a beast, are eliminated.

"Third floor, watch your step, please."

Mrs. Moody led the way down the hall, helpfully pointed to the brass plate on a door, and opened it. They stepped into a large room whose wall of windows faced the park. The furniture was antique French reproduction—a gracefully curved desk, a reading table, a pair of softly upholstered reading chairs, and a nice big bed. There was room in it for several bears.

"Your next interview isn't until noon. You'll have some time to rest up a bit." Mrs. Moody was opening a refrigerated bar with the room key.

The bear peered excitedly in, and removed the various snacks, along with a bottle of champagne.

"You're hungry?" asked Mrs. Moody. "Just call down." She handed him the room service menu.

He saw with pleasure that they had cooked bird, choice pieces of cow, and salmon. "One of each," he said, and stretched out on the bed.

Somewhat startled, Mrs. Moody hesitated at the door, with the feeling that perhaps her young author could continue to benefit by her presence. She sensed something vaguely inexperienced about him, and she wanted to be sure he was comfortable. "When you need laundry done, you call down and housekeeping will pick it up."

"I change my underwear every day," said the bear proudly.

The bear's meal came to him on a wheeled table with a white tablecloth on it and a warming cabinet underneath, from which his three meals were served. "You're expecting guests, sir?" asked the waiter.

"It's just me," smiled the bear, tucking a napkin into his collar. He gave the waiter a hundred-dollar tip, because he liked everyone to be happy and because he wanted to keep things moving smoothly on the food front.

"Enjoy your meal, sir," said the waiter sincerely.

The bear commenced eating beside the windows, gazing out toward the park. There was roast duck on his plate and ducks floating in the pond outside. He nodded in approval. Very convenient. They just go over and kill one. He wondered—should I volunteer my services? I'll suggest it later.

Bears are congenial but solitary creatures and he was

content eating alone this way in a nice comfy chair. He now knew that bittersweet thoughts about his forest life were distortions and served only to undermine his present happiness. A bear had to live in the moment. He ate one meal, belched gently, and started in on the second. Your omnivore on tour, digesting nicely.

The telephone rang and he stretched out a paw.

"*Hal, it's Bettina. Is everything all right there? Are you comfortable?*"

"Sure."

"*I saw the interview with Sandy Kincaid. You were wonderful.*"

"They wash my underwear."

"*What?*"

"When it gets dirty, they wash it. Well, good-bye."

He ate several desserts and then turned slowly in his chair, facing back into the room. The excellent housekeeping pleased him. Crisp clean sheets have it all over pine boughs when it comes to nap time.

He got up, stretched out on the bed, and closed his eyes. A lovely heaviness rolled in, the dreaminess of the bear in repose. He saw bright little champagne bottles dancing around, their transparent forms filled with sparkling liquids that swirled him toward sleep.

Arthur Bramhall lay sleeping in his den. He had dreams. He dreamed of bears; their great dark forms rubbed against him, then led him down forest trails.

"I'm downstairs," said a female voice.

"I'm upstairs."

"Hal, it's Julie Moody. It's time for your next interview. Do you need help getting ready?"

"I can tie my shoes," he said with dignity, and hung up. Does she think a bear can't dress himself?

Fly zipped. Now the clip-on tie, what a device. The man who invented it was a genius.

Key, money, candy bar. I'm ready.

He made a few territorial scratch marks on the wallpaper and left the room.

"Hal, you're a blast," said Dave Drover, the fast-talking host of *Driving with Drover*, a Boston rush-hour radio show broadcast over the most powerful radio station in the Northeast. "I mean it, you're a breath of fresh air in the airwaves. Okay, let's take a break for the weather and I'll be right back with my guest, Hal Jam, author of *Destiny and Desire.*" Dave Drover removed his earphones and swiveled in his chair toward his guest. "The switchboard is lit up. People want to talk to you, pal." Drover took a quick sniff from the inside of his French shirt cuff, in which his daily ration of cocaine was stashed. When the diamonds hit his brain, his mind raced into regions of speech so swift that no one, not even he, could follow them, and he became momentarily silent. When the weather report was finished, Drover signaled for the commercial and slipped his earphones back on. The bear sat across from him, in front of another microphone, with only a vague understanding of the part he was playing in the rush-hour radio broadcast. But he was deeply impressed by the speed of Dave Drover's speech. He yearned to talk fast like that, to have words dancing on the end of his tongue, to send them spinning out into the air, light, nimble, in a bubbling stream.

"Welcome back, everyone, you're driving with Drover at half past the hour. My guest is Hal Jam, his book is *Destiny and Desire*, and he's a fantastic writer, and an original thinker, as I think you'll agree. Hal, simple question, please forgive it: How did you get started in writing?"

The bear wanted desperately to match the sparkle of Drover's speech, to twinkle and bubble, to dance in the fountain of sound, and he tried to recall what really got him started, what first drew him to the world of humanity. "Garbage."

Drover liked sharp, one-word answers from his guests, for that sent the ball quickly back to him, and he was born to talk: "You looked at what was around, you saw it was garbage, and you thought *I can do better*. Not surprising. And then?"

"A man put a book under a tree."

"Simple and poetic. And you were that man."

"I was watching."

"Were you ever. In your book you've got some of the most telling observations I've ever seen. This book is a manual for everyone who's confused about relationships between the sexes, and that's undoubtedly one of the reasons it's so popular, and there's someone on the line who wants to talk about it. Go ahead, you're driving with Drover."

"Yes, my name's Marcia. I haven't read the book. You said it's a sex manual?"

"In a manner of speaking, Marcia," answered Dave Drover. "What's your question?"

"I want to know if your guest thinks people who live in the country have better orgasms. Because maybe I should move there."

"I don't think they've got a way of monitoring that, Marcia, but let's ask our guest. Hal, what do you think?"

The bear leaned toward his own microphone. He didn't know what they were talking about, so he said, "Sugar."

"Right on, Hal, it's sweet wherever you get it," said

197

Dave Drover, "and good luck with your move, Marcia." Drover smiled appreciatively toward his quiet guest. The guy knew whose show it was.

In New York City, Bettina was listening on her office radio. She turned to Gadson. "Tell me Hal isn't a phenomenon."

"Well, sales *are* going through the roof."

Bettina strode back and forth in front of her window, her eyes on the East Side skyline. "He cuts through the communication barriers that inhibit the rest of us."

"Yes, you can't say he's inhibited."

"But he's basically unassuming. That's why he's doing so well. He doesn't threaten people with complicated ideas."

"For the longest time I thought he was brain-damaged," admitted Gadson.

Vinal Pinette sat in front of his living room stove, staring at the flames dancing behind the stove's glass window. His dog lay beside him, chin on his paws, tail thumping rhythmically.

"It don't do to fool with nature," said Pinette.

The dog looked up, intent upon the molasses cookie Pinette was dunking into his tea. The dog observed that there were more of them on a nearby plate, and a cookie right about now would be appreciated. Should none be forthcoming, he'd go back to licking his balls, which always had a soothing effect on him.

"We just have to wait it out and watch," said Pinette, bringing the tea-soaked cookie to his lips.

The dog's tail thumped harder, and he gave his most eloquent look, the one with cookie written all over it.

Pinette turned toward the window and gazed out to the drifts of snow starting to bury the junked cars in his field. He missed Art Bramhall, missed talking with him by the stove, missed keeping watch with him over the slow procession of winter days. "Art's a good feller. I hope we see him again."

The cookie is the natural food of dogs, said the dog, and emphasized the point with a pathetic look that was meant to show the pitiful results of cookie depletion in his system.

"You already had four," replied Pinette.

It's winter, I'm a dog, all I've got to keep me going is licking my balls and the love of cookies.

Pinette reached to the plate, tossed one, and the brown morsel was trapped in the dog's flashing jaws. In one gulp it was gone.

It's a pity I can't slow that process down, reflected the dog as he stared at the floor. If I broke the cookie up into little pieces I could savor the experience. But somehow in the passion of the moment, I lose control.

"Secret Service guys," said the Ritz Carlton elevator man to the bear, drawing attention to the several serious-looking young men in dark suits, standing stiffly in the lobby. The bear sniffed toward them and smelled the tension trickling down their armpits.

He looked out toward the street. People were shouting and holding signs, and it made him nervous. He was glad to be on his way back to his room, but as he was lumbering into the elevator, the next elevator opened, a dominant male stepped out, and everyone in the lobby turned toward him.

"Have a nice day, Mr. Vice President," said the elevator man.

The vice president wished the elevator man the same. He was surrounded by staff, and Boston politicians. The bear smelled adrenaline and noted how the figures around the vice president were chattering like overwrought squirrels defending their nuts.

The bear didn't know what a vice president was. This was because he was a bear. He wondered if he ought to challenge this dominant male. Maybe pick him up and shake him a little, just to make the point about who was top bear in this lobby. But there are plenty of females to go around, reflected the genial bear as he watched the women striking mating poses for the vice president and making mating signals with their eyes, lips, fingers. They were in pretty coats and their hair was shiny and smelled good and their legs were shiny too, but after all, I've already mated twice this year. I'll leave the field to this other dominant male.

With this convivial gesture, he turned back toward the elevator door. But as he did, another strong smell floated in on him, a smell like the one a coyote puts out when he's stalking. He turned around and sniffed the air. Separating the various currents filling the lobby, he determined that the coyote smell was drifting down from a male who was descending the staircase from the tearoom on the second floor. The bear watched him carefully, for that funky smell meant a kill was about to take place.

The bear had spent a day and a night in the hotel, which made it his territory, and while he didn't mind sharing the women with another dominant male, he couldn't allow overt displays of aggression to go unchallenged. He liked this hotel, the food was good, and they'd washed his underwear and returned it nicely folded in a plastic bag. If anybody was going to get aggressive, it would be him.

The aggressive male stepped off the stairs and edged his way toward the vice president. His name was Wilfred

Gagunkas and he was preparing to blow up the vice president and himself. Gagunkas's selfless desire to die, and take everybody in the lobby with him, was fueled by the terrible knowledge that a former Amtrak station in Boston was being converted into a massive crematorium for disposing of those men, women, and innocent children who resisted the One World invasion. Highway signs in and around Boston had already been marked with stickers by U.N. troops, orange for confiscation of nearby facilities, blue to indicate cremation areas, green for helicopter landing sites. Rolled up in Gagunkas's back pocket was the latest intelligence issue of *The Constitutionalist*, which contained vital information on California earthquakes. Gagunkas had been astounded to learn that six of the biggest earthquakes in recent history had taken place in conjunction with abortion- or homosexual-related events. Shit like that *had* to stop.

The Constitutionalist also detailed how the IRS is building gigantic silos in Kansas to imprison loyal Americans. Any concerned citizen trying to get near these silos is killed immediately by black-uniformed troops. However, the Rockefellers are allowed to go there without any problems. This information, and so much more, was circulating in Gagunkas's overloaded brain.

Gagunkas knew for a fact that the United Nations had put Russian soldiers on U.S. soil and that the entire U.S. Air Force was run by Austrians. People looked at you like you were nuts when you told them the One World Police State was already here, but the Russkies were performing maneuvers in Idaho. There were Chinese tank crews in Arizona. Yid bankers were financing a Super Tunnel from Siberia to Alaska. There was a secret elevator in the White House that went seventeen stories underground, to the command bunker of the One World Government, and the vice president rode it every day to receive his marching orders.

Now, thought Gagunkas, a blow for freedom. I'll show these liberal pukes how a real man dies!

The bear calmly bopped Gagunkas on top of the head, and Gagunkas fell to the floor. As he did so, the voices of the Secret Service agents erupted.

"Incident at one o'clock! Take cover and evacuate!"

Agents grabbed the vice president, shielding him from the crowd with their bodies and moving him toward the door. Vice-presidential staffers flung themselves gallantly under lobby furniture as the Secret Service men cranked their weapons.

"Here," said the bear, pointing down at Gagunkas.

Several agents hurried over and, very carefully, opened Gagunkas's jacket. "He's covered with plastique. That's a detonator on his belt. We'd have been chopped meat."

"My territory," explained the bear.

The agents handcuffed Gagunkas where he lay unconscious, and called for the city's bomb squad.

"If you'd step this way, sir," said an agent to the bear, taking out his notebook. "How did you know he was strapped?"

The bear tapped his nose.

"You just smelled it," smiled the agent. "That's how it is sometimes."

"Well, good-bye," said the bear, and stepped toward his elevator.

The vice president's schedule did not allow him to personally thank the bear. But a note was made of the bear's name, and the slow wheels of government were set in motion.

"Hal stopped an assassination attempt on the vice president!" Bettina burst into Gadson's office. "He was on CNN just now. Christ, what a break." Bettina gingerly stepped past the life-size replica of Barton Balfour III. "Of course, the reporters couldn't get much out of him."

"He down-played it?"

"He looked like he'd forgotten it. How could you forget saving the vice president's life?"

"Einstein couldn't take public transportation," said Gadson. "He'd forget where he was going."

"He *is* a sort of Einstein, isn't he? I mean, on another wavelength or something. I suppose I can work that angle."

"It seems to me as if Hal has worked the angles for you."

Arthur Bramhall slept his deep sleep undisturbed. Vinal Pinette snowshoed through the woods every day and quietly checked on him. The fur-bearing woman went with him a few times, but never actually entered the cave. She didn't like to intrude on anyone's personal boundaries. She was even circumspect with her sheep.

The bear sat surrounded by tall stacks of his book, which the bookstore in Philadelphia hoped to sell that day. It pleased book lovers that he took the time to write his name clearly, rather than just dashing off the swift, disdainful bit of illegibility that some writers put onto the title page of their books.

"Would you please sign this one for Bob?" asked the woman standing before him now.

"How do you spell it?" asked the bear.

"Spell what?"

"Bob."

"Oh, the usual way," laughed the woman, and then saw that Jam was waiting for her, his pen poised over the book. "B–O–B," she said in some confusion.

The bear mouthed the letters silently as he wrote them, *B–O–B,* and then mouthed his own name as he wrote it, *J–A–M.*

His media escort in Philadelphia was Adele Nofsacker. Adele was inclined toward hysteria, and when she saw how slowly he wrote, she knew that watching him would be unbearable, so she'd gotten him to shorten his signature to *Jam*, which he liked, because you couldn't do better than Jam.

Now she walked to the front of the store, where the manager was beaming over the turnout for Jam's appearance. "He's caught on like wildfire, hasn't he? Of course, saving the vice president hasn't hurt."

While the manager was talking to Adele, an advance *New York Times Book Review* arrived. Adele quickly turned to the best-seller list. Hal Jam's book had hit number one.

Adele carried the newspaper over to Jam's table and laid it in front of him. "You did it," she said.

The bear looked to where she pointed, then looked up at Adele.

"You're number one," she said.

"I'm Jam," he said insistently.

The signing went well, as did the interviews that afternoon. The bear now knew that the blinding lights of a TV studio held no menace, that no one lay in wait for him in the surrounding darkness. Prior to each interview he insisted on a supply of Cheesy Things, which he ate during the interview. On returning to the Latham Hotel with Adele Nofsacker that night, he was approached in the lobby by a rotund gentleman carrying a briefcase. "Mr. Jam?"

The bear looked at the briefcase hopefully. "Do you have a novel in there?"

The man appeared puzzled, and Adele Nofsacker

took over. "Mr. Jam has had a long day, and needs to rest." Adele's sacred vocation was protecting her writers, and Hal Jam needed more than most; the poor man was so gentle, so accommodating, he'd never get any peace if she let autograph seekers hound him into the night.

"I'm from the Cheesy Things Company. I'm here to make Mr. Jam an offer."

The bear's ears lifted. "You have Cheesy Things?"

The man opened his briefcase and handed the bear a bag. "We were delighted to learn how much you enjoy them."

"You'll have to contact Mr. Jam's lawyers," said Adele. "Come along, Hal."

"Please," said the Cheesy Things man. "I flew in from Wisconsin especially to see Mr. Jam. Surely he can spare five minutes."

"Tomorrow," said Adele. "Mr. Jam is very tired."

"Excuse me," said the man from Cheesy Things. "You are?"

"Adele Nofsacker."

"Ms. Nofsacker, I know you've both had a long day, and I don't wish to intrude." The Cheesy Things man edged a little closer, trying to intrude, but the bear was walking away, nibbling the product, which bore a close resemblance, visually and chemically, to Styrofoam packing peanuts, coated egg-yolk yellow. He pressed the elevator button as the Cheesy Things man moved in alongside him, with Adele Nofsacker on the other side.

"Mr. Jam, Cheesy Things is offering you money."

"Call us in the morning," said Adele Nofsacker.

The elevator door opened and the Cheesy Things man forced his way in beside them. "We'd like you to go on eating our Cheesy Things on your tour, wherever you go. For which we'll pay you two hundred and fifty thousand dollars."

"You have to be joking," said Adele Nofsacker. "Mr. Jam is a distinguished American author, not a basketball player. He doesn't lend his name to any product except his own books."

The elevator was now rising. The bear continued to nibble his crispy, puffy treat. As one who'd found the cellulose in wasps' nests palatable, he was right at home with a mouthful of Cheesy Things.

"But look at him," said the man from Cheesy Things. "He loves our product."

"He's not endorsing it," said Adele Nofsacker, staring at the elevator panel as the floors lit up.

"Look," said the Cheesy Things man as the elevator door opened, "I can go a little higher."

"You've gone as high as you're going," said Adele. "Mr. Jam has an early flight tomorrow and he needs his sleep."

"If he has an early flight how am I supposed to talk to him tomorrow?"

"That's your problem," said Adele.

The bear walked behind them, shaking the Cheesy Things bag into his mouth. He'd said a lot of words today and was pleased with himself.

"All right, we'll give him three hundred thousand."

Adele Nofsacker inserted the key into the bear's door. "I don't think you understand. Mr. Jam is not interested."

"A case of our product is delivered to each of his hotels along the way, and all he has to do is eat from a single bag on the air, or display it in some other natural and convenient way. For which we'll give him three hundred and fifty thousand dollars."

Adele Nofsacker gave the Cheesy Things man a look of contempt. "Mr. Jam declines your offer."

The bear passed through the opened door, which Adele Nofsacker tried to close on the Cheesy Things man, but he inserted his briefcase at the last moment.

"All right, all right, we'll make it four hundred thousand. That's a fair offer, because we're not talking a long-term endorsement here, only the length of the tour."

Adele Nofsacker stared at the Cheesy Things man as if he were a carpet beetle. "Half a million."

"Deal." The Cheesy Things man opened his briefcase and whipped out a contract. "And by the way, would you consider working for Cheesy Things?"

"We'll talk later," said Adele.

Vinal Pinette sat down on his old iron bed. He wore a frayed knit cap to keep his bald head warm, and his dentures were in a glass, smiling at the faded wallpaper. Outside, the snow piled up to the edge of the windowsill, and the moonlight shone on the rounded snowbank and the heavily burdened trees. "Art's like a son to me," remarked Pinette to his dog, who was on the floor beside the bed.

The dog looked up, hoping for a last little morsel to round off the day, a good-night wiener, perhaps.

A bare light bulb hung above the bed, still burning. Pinette reached up and turned it off. The moonlit window became the brightest spot in the room. "Art, my boy," he said, "I hope you're keeping well."

The dog walked out of the bedroom, his nails making soft clicking sounds on the warped pine floorboards. He walked into the kitchen and stared into his dish. It was empty, of course. Still, it never hurt to check.

He had a noisy slurp of water and then curled himself behind the kitchen stove. Sighing, he wrapped his tail over his nose and closed his eyes. After a few minutes he was asleep, chasing wieners through his dreams. He snapped at them so violently he woke himself up.

Only a dream, he said, and sighed again, the ancient sigh of the dog by the fire when wieners are in short supply.

When the bear and his Chicago escort, Will Elder, entered the Channel 7 green room, the Reverend Norbert Sinkler was also waiting there. Elder introduced the two best-selling authors. "Reverend Sinkler, Hal Jam. You're both high on the charts this week."

"Well, well," said Sinkler, his eyes lighting up. The Reverend Sinkler wanted to *reach out*. He was not accustomed to socializing with moderates, but if he was going to make a run for the presidency, he needed them. "I'm delighted to meet you, sir, delighted indeed."

The bear shook Reverend Sinkler's hand, and the reverend was pleased to see that it wasn't some wishy-washy fag grip, but a fine, manly handshake.

"I read your book," said the bear, because his publicist had told him to always say that to his fellow authors so no one's feelings would ever be hurt.

"You have? Why, that gives me pleasure, Mr. . . . er . . . Jam, it certainly does. Especially because I enjoyed *your* book enormously." Reverend Sinkler hadn't known of its existence until a moment ago, but his publicity director had also counseled him that it was important to say he'd read the book of any other writer he met.

"I can see you two have a lot to talk about," said Elder, and eased himself out of the room.

Sinkler gazed at the bear with the benevolent gaze he shone on all human beings, so that they might know that he loved them. The bear gazed back, sniffing the reverend. He got faint traces of two-hundred-dollar cologne. He also smelled Pan-Cake makeup, and it smelled edible. He leaned over, held the reverend by the shoulders, and licked his face. It had a buttery sort of flavor.

Sinkler attempted to draw back, but a fine, manly grip held him firm. Is he a Frenchie? wondered Sinkler, then decided it had to be something like that, for the man was a best-seller, not a pervert. "Thank you for your sincere display of emotion, sir. I see we're together on that long and shining road that leads to everlasting brotherhood."

The producer entered. "Reverend, we're ready for you now."

Sinkler pivoted like a top as the long and shining road of telecommunications rose up before him. "Time to proclaim at the crossroads," he said with a loving smile.

The bear remained in the green room, eating his Cheesy Things. A wall monitor carried the show, and he saw the reverend talking to the show's host. He looked around for a remote with which to change channels, but there was none. When an assistant producer walked in, the bear pointed at the monitor and said, "Cartoons."

"You can say that again," said the assistant producer, eyeing the reverend on the screen.

The bear nodded, eyes still on the monitor, where the reverend was speaking in the cadence of an earlier, more primitive America. The bear was impressed with the reverend's sonorous drone.

The assistant producer shook his head. "It's frightening to think he could be our next president."

"I want to talk like him," said the bear.

The assistant producer chuckled. "We all do. He's worth a hundred million."

This figure was meaningless to the bear, as he'd gone from being a bear to being a millionaire with no stops in between. But he still couldn't speak in long, droning sentences like the man on the screen.

When his turn came, he gave his typical interview, which confounded the show's host, delighted the cameramen, and lit up the switchboards. Reverend Sinkler watched on the television in his limo, amazed by the simplicity of his fellow best-seller. "I'm going to have Hal Jam down to Godland," he said to Craig Sudekum, a Christian publicist.

Sudekum cleared his throat diplomatically. "The man embraces extramarital sex in his book, Reverend."

"We've got to move with the times, Sudekum."

"Always risky, Reverend."

"I'm *reaching out.*"

"I recognize that, Reverend." Craig Sudekum was the gray eminence behind Norbert Sinkler. Sinkler had the charisma and the common touch, but Sudekum had the brains, and had carried this big, dumb Bible-walloper from obscurity to the threshold of the White House.

"Hal Jam's warm and sincere," said Sinkler. "He doesn't use big words. He doesn't make you feel like a dumbbell." Reverend Sinkler stared out the window toward the street. "I like Hal. I think my congregation would like him too."

"If kept off fornicational topics, Reverend."

"He's looking for readers, Sudekum, same as I am. We'll keep him off fornication and show him off to the moderates. I *need* moderates, and this man Jam will be my first. He's actually read my book."

"Yessir. Do you wish me to contact him?"

"You do that." Reverend Sinkler got on the intercom to the driver. "I'm seeing black faces. Lower the gold."

"Yessir," said the driver, and pressed a button on the control console. The fourteen-carat gold crucifix that served as a hood ornament on the Godland limo lowered itself electronically into the hood and sank out of sight.

. . .

Reverend Sinkler and the bear dined together in the Pump Room of the Omni Ambassador. Jacket and tie were required. The bear was wearing his tweed suit and clip-on tie; Reverend Sinkler was in a navy blazer with gold buttons, to match the tiny, eighteen-carat crucifix fixed to his Armani tie.

The reverend lifted his wineglass and sipped judiciously. "You'll be at the top of the show, nothing too formal, just some light conversation. I have to tell you up front that sex can't be one of those topics, unless it's family oriented. Will that be a problem?"

"No problem," said the bear. Bettina had instructed him to say this whenever anybody on the tour asked him if he could do something. *Do it all, Hal. All publicity is good. Just say* no problem.

"I'm happy to hear you say that, Hal, happy indeed. I knew it wouldn't be hard for a man of your character and faith to modify his presentation."

"No problem," repeated the bear. He was eating Pump Room chicken fricassee, and his mood was a contented one. I've got the largest territory of any bear in the world, he said to himself. None of the others come close. Without fear of contradiction I can say there's not a bear alive who wouldn't want to be eating chicken fricassee right now. But would their table manners be as well developed? Would they have their napkin tucked under their chin? Would their paw be out of the soup or dangling inside it? These gains are not won easily. Another bear in this situation would be slobbering and farting. He might drop a turd alongside his chair, as a warning that everything on the table is his. I've resisted. It hasn't been easy. But it was necessary.

"I'd like to change gears here, Hal, and talk some politics. I'm not seeking office, mind you, but there's a ground swell of folks who think I should take a shot at the White House. What would you think of my candidacy?"

The reverend had gestured with his fork as he said this, and the bear assumed that candidacy must be something like fricassee. He lifted his own fork. "Sounds tasty."

"Well, well," said Sinkler with a satisfied smile. "That's very good to hear, sir, very good indeed." What in hell does Sudekum know about politics? thought the Reverend Sinkler to himself. I *knew* Jam was ready to swing to the right. "We're moving fast here, Hal, but I think great movements always do. Would you endorse my candidacy on the air?"

"No problem," said the bear.

"That's wonderful, Hal, and most gratifying. Since we're moving right along, I don't mind telling you I think I can do something for this country. Because a country is like a congregation." Why, that's not half-bad, thought Sinkler to himself, and made a note to give that line to his speech writers for further development. *A country is like a congregation. A country is a congregation.* "I can promise you this, Hal. Nobody will ever be able to accuse me of pulling my pants down with some secretary in a motel room."

The bear looked down into his lap, checking as he often did, on the correctness of his own pants. "I have mine on right."

"Of course you do, and so do I." Reverend Sinkler had wrestled with the devil of lust on several notable occasions, but had always managed to keep his pants on. There was at this moment a woman seated at the table across from him with her half-bare tits squeezed up over the neck of her dress. Tits a man could lose an election over. The reverend looked back toward Jam. "We're all human."

"I'm trying to be," said the bear.

"Very well put, my friend. Very well indeed. And I'm trying too."

"You too?" asked the bear.

"Me too, Hal. I won't pretend I haven't known animal lust." Reverend Sinkler felt a strange bond with Hal Jam. The man didn't sit in judgment of you, and for this reason Reverend Sinkler felt he could share with him openly. "I've got thirty-seven good-looking women singing in a choir behind me every Sunday. But I don't take advantage of my position."

"I usually do it from behind," said the bear.

"They're bonding," said Will Elder at a nearby table.

He was speaking on a cellular phone, long-distance to New York.

"*He's bonding with Norbert Sinkler?*" Bettina was at home in alphabet city, her workday done, but Will Elder had instructions to call her if Hal Jam got himself in trouble.

"Sinkler's invited him to Godland."

"*And he accepted?*"

"He's going to appear on the Godland Prayer and Shopping Network."

"*How the hell did this happen?*"

"They hit it off."

"*There goes the National Book Award. The Cheesy Things endorsement was bad enough.*"

"Writers on tour are adults in diapers."

"*When is he supposed to go on the air with Sinkler?*"

"Tomorrow."

"*Isn't there anything you can do, Will?*"

"I'll do my best, but short of locking him in the closet . . ."

Godland was ten miles out of Chicago, and the bear arrived in a Godland limo. The bear had no concept of religion. He was here for the candidacy, which he pictured in a creamy sauce with tender little peas floating in it.

223

Norbert Sinkler himself greeted the bear as the limo pulled up in front of the main building. This building was dubbed Kingdom Come Hall and was a study in giantism worthy of the Third Reich.

"Welcome, Hal," said Reverend Sinkler. "God Himself told me this morning how happy He was that you were coming."

The bear squinted up into the bright winter sky. Sunlight shined on the dome of Kingdom Come Hall and on the fluttering flag of the Everlasting Miracle Ministry, Limited Liability. He sniffed the air for chicken candidacy, but the only smell was that of french fries coming from the surrounding Godland shopping mall.

Norbert Sinkler took his guest by the elbow and led him toward the entrance to Kingdom Come Hall. "We're proud of our place in the American landscape, Hal," said Sinkler, gesturing at the colorful gingerbread designs of the shops on the streets radiating out from the holy center. The bear thought the architecture was pretty nice too. This was because he was a bear.

Reverend Sinkler led him into the hall, which echoed with their footsteps. The bear stared up at the domed ceiling. It was the highest ceiling he'd ever seen, with pretty paintings on it, of Norbert Sinkler and a longhaired, bearded man leading people toward the clouds.

"All of this was built by prayer," said Sinkler.

The bear's nose began to twitch. He was getting hungry. "Let's have your candidacy."

"We're working on it round the clock, Hal. Mailings. Telephone solicitations. Major advertising. God *will* be in the White House." Reverend Sinkler imagined himself on inauguration day, taking the oath of office, his resonant tones filling the hearts and minds of the world. That's why he needed Jam, and others like him, moderates who were finding their way toward redemption.

"I'd like your candidacy now," said the bear.

"So would I." Sinkler was moved by his guest's earnestness. "But these things take time."

The bear nodded, and his tongue went over his snout again, in loving anticipation of those little peas in sauce.

Sinkler led the way into the backstage area of the hall, threading through lengths of electric cable. The bear was taken in tow by the makeup people and then handed over to the assistant director. Through the curtains could be heard the audience of several thousand believers in Norbert Sinkler's version of reality, who would join hearts with the millions more who watched the Christian Prayer and Shopping Network at home.

The assistant director led the bear onstage to the guest chair, and Reverend Sinkler went to his podium. The orchestra settled in, and the choir members came onstage, in long red robes.

The bear's nose immediately pointed toward the thirty-seven women in their long red robes. Fine-smelling bunch of females, he said to himself. Gives a bear the urge to make little bears, just the way nature planned it, more or less.

The cameras swung into position, the director's signal came from the control booth, and the show's theme music began.

The cloud of scents emanating from the thirty-seven robes whispered and danced in the bear's nose. He'd gotten a taste for human females, and they were the best. He knew he was being a bad bear, but a desperate urge ran through him, to bite, display, challenge. Could be some trouble up ahead, but a bear only lives once.

The women of the choir looked at him in nervous fascination. The male guests who came on the Prayer and Shopping Network talked about family values. This man was sniffing the choir, as if . . . well, it was too disturbing to think about, but as if he had his nose *up there*.

"My dear friends, welcome." Norbert Sinkler bowed his head toward the audience, and on cue the choir began to sing softly in the background, their eyes still taking sidelong glances toward the guest.

"My friends, I've had God's blessing on me today, and I've heard His word in my ear. God said to me, 'Norbert, give those folks the biggest, most loving welcome you can. Open your heart to them, so that they can open their hearts to God . . .' "

The bear's heart was opening to the lovely ladies. Their song was sweet, and their scent was going up his nose into his brain, commanding him with a primordial command, to conquer all that female flesh, to frolic in its moist scent. Yes, he said to himself, yes, *yes*.

Norbert Sinkler's back was to the choir as he plunged on with his sermon, feeling it was going to be a *rouser*.

The choir continued their song, for they were professionals, but the burly guest was striding directly toward them with a wild expression on his face.

". . . God said, 'Give those folks the good news, Norbert,' and I said, 'I will, Lord, I surely will.' "

The bear had mounted the red-carpeted steps in front of the choir and now he let out a roar, just to make sure everyone knew who these females belonged to.

What in the hell, thought Norbert Sinkler, and fell into stunned silence.

The bear roared again, and threw his paws in the air, in his species' ancient gesture of territorial sovereignty.

The roar reverberated throughout the auditorium, and several of the faithful in the front row were moved by it, to the marrow of their bones. "Hallelujah!" they cried, and rose to their feet, throwing *their* arms into the air.

"Glory, glory, *glory!*"

The entire row stood up, joining the show's dynamic guest in his praise of the Lord.

At that moment, a word came into the bewildered preacher's ear. It was not the word of god, but that of the director, over Sinkler's ear receiver. *"Go with it, Reverend."*

The Reverend Sinkler dutifully held his arms out toward the audience, a smile pasted on his lips. "You feel it, my friends, you feel the *message* . . ."

The bear too turned toward the audience, stunned by the sound of hundreds, and then thousands, of people shouting as one.

"Hallelujah! Hallelujah!"

He roared back, louder than before, his roar of roars, the roar of primacy in the forest.

Now, *there's* a Christian, thought the audience, answering with their own roar.

The bear forgot about the ladies of the choir. The sound of so many human voices blended together was astounding. Humanity could do this, could merge with a single purpose. It was how they'd discovered popcorn and panties. And the incredible thing was—he was leading them! He roared again, just to be sure. They roared back, everyone coming to their feet and waving their arms in the air, and he knew—he was in control of the buzz.

Bettina Quint charged into the back of the studio

and saw, with horror, that she was too late. Hal had caused a riot.

Then she saw Will Elder, who had done his best as promised, and was in the back of the auditorium, manning a table piled high with copies of *Destiny and Desire*. And then the stampede began, one audience member after another hurrying to buy the book of this great charismatic leader who was rocking the rafters of Kingdom Come Hall.

"Be a good boy, Hal," said Bettina at the airport. She and Will Elder had accompanied him to the Delta waiting area. His bags had been sent through. He carried a briefcase filled with Cheesy Things.

"We're going to change the ground rules slightly," continued Bettina. "If anyone asks you to do something, call me first."

"Sure," said the bear.

"Why do I think you're not listening to me?"

"Delta is now boarding all first-class passengers to Dallas . . ."

"Well, good-bye," said the bear, and walked toward the loading gate, ticket in his paw.

Arthur Bramhall woke in his dark cave. He felt the pine boughs beneath him and the walls of rocks surrounding him. Springtime was a long way off, and the pull of sleep was strong, to roll over and curl back into his boughs. But something said *get up*.

He crawled in the dark toward the thin crust of snow that covered the entrance to the cave. He scraped through the snow and stuck his head out into a dying winter landscape. The sun was low in the sky. He squinted against the brightness and continued scraping the snow away with harsh, pawing movements. He was hungry, hungrier than he'd ever been. He was hungry for food and for life.

He pried open the back window of a restaurant. Muffled snorts and grunts came from him as he pushed himself in over the window ledge and landed clumsily on the floor. He rocked his head back and forth, sniffing the darkened kitchen. He let out a grunt of recognition and made his way toward the refrigerator. He opened it and pulled out a pie, which he pawed hungrily, stuffing pieces of it in his mouth. After finishing the pie he started on a chocolate layer cake. He felt himself to be very clever in having found these items. Beside this, he had no other thoughts.

As he ate, his nose was drawn to a parcel in the refrigerator—a fish wrapped in newspaper. He tore open the newspaper and was preparing to bite into the raw fish when a light, as dim as the one in the refrigerator, went on in his mind. Where the paper curved around the fish's head, he caught sight of a familiar title: *Destiny and Desire*. He lifted the fish aside and carefully smoothed out the newspaper. The title was at the top of the best-seller list. Suddenly a remembrance of things past came to him as they had to Proust, in exquisite detail: with Proust it had been a cookie dipped in tea that brought back the flavor of the past. With Bramhall it was a fish wrapped in newspaper, but the chemistry was the same—there was the memory of his beloved book over which he'd labored with such devotion. Every sentence of it was burning in his mind and he knew that he'd been screwed.

But by whom? he wondered, and then he recalled the tracks beneath the tree.

"Screwed by a bear?" His voice sounded foreign to him as it echoed in the empty restaurant kitchen. Human speech had slept in him, but now he was caught again in the web of words—their meanings and the sorrow they could articulate. "Screwed by a bear!" he cried, and ripped the newspaper in half, straight down through the best-seller list, after which he hurled the fish at the wall.

His stomach was rumbling from the pie and cake he'd greedily shoved down it; a bear could handle such gorging, but Bramhall was swiftly shaking off his bearness. "God almighty," he said as he caught sight of himself in the reflected light on the window—a hairy, naked creature with pine needles and twigs in its gnarled beard. He tried to neaten himself up, then realized it was dangerous to do so here. He had to get away before he was caught and hauled off to jail or an insane asylum.

He went out through the broken window, grunting as he did so, which gave him another shock. The bear in him wasn't quite dead yet.

"I've studied your case, Mr. Bramhall." Eaton Magoon looked across the desk at his prospective client.

"Well?" growled Arthur Bramhall, who, with much difficulty, was returning to civilization. The suit he wore was splitting at the seams. It had fit him perfectly once, but he now had an inch of hair all over his body, and his neck had grown noticeably thicker.

Through the window behind lawyer Magoon, the town clock was visible, its hands permanently stopped. Beyond the clock was the Feed and Seed store. The lettering on the sign was faded and old, like much of northern Maine. "I'm just a small-town lawyer, Mr. Bramhall, and you've got a lot going against you."

"But it's my book," growled Bramhall. He'd been unable to get the gravelly sound out of his voice, and every sentence he spoke ended in a soft howl, like a dog with worms.

"There's no carbon of it," continued Magoon, "which leaves us with no proof that in fact you are the author of *Destiny and Desire.*"

"Ask Vinal Pinette. He'll tell you I was working on a book."

"Yes, but what book? Vinal Pinette can barely read."

"He's an honest man."

"Honest but illiterate. He'd make a good witness if this were a case of a stolen cow."

"I wrote *Destiny and Desire*."

"I believe you, Mr. Bramhall. But will a judge? Will a jury? May I be straightforward?"

"Certainly."

"Your appearance is against you. You don't look like an author."

"What do I look like?"

"Frankly, you look like a bear."

The bear's tour ended in Southern California, whose lushness was like nothing he'd ever encountered before. He took an early morning walk on the grounds of the Hotel Bel Air. The tropical trees with their gigantic roots and branches filled the air with a sultry power. He wandered down the path to the pond, in which a pair of the hotel's trademark swans were swimming. They were pampered creatures, and when the bear looked at them he could not help drooling. Bear drool is aromatic and the swans were shocked. Who was this barbarian? How had he gotten into their hotel? They disdainfully turned their tail feathers toward him and paddled away. The bear charged, paws thumping on the grass. The swans twisted their long necks around in horror, then raced very inelegantly up the far bank into the bushes.

The bear skidded to a stop on the edge of the pond and looked back over his shoulder to see if he'd been observed. I've got to hold back on the woodland instincts here. Could be a world of misunderstandings if I ate those birds.

Attempting a casual air, he climbed up out of the swan garden, to another path. It was lined with moist, exotic flowers; fountains shaped like animal heads spouted water from their mouths. He crossed the dining terrace beneath a canopy of branches which held masses of blue blossoms. Females were already lying on loungers beside the pool, with a shoestring between their buns. He paused, and the young pool attendant said, "Can I set you up in a chair, sir?"

"I'm looking at the buns."

"Certainly, sir."

The bear helped himself to a banana from the fruit basket set out for the bathers. Morning sunlight glittered on the pool, and tropical birds sang in the trees. Might be nice to take a little dip, he said to himself.

He removed his hotel robe and took several slow, graceful steps toward the water, then launched himself and hit the water with a tremendous splash, sending waves surging up over the edges of the pool.

With the cloudless California sky above him, he paddled peacefully along. As he paddled, he kept his eye out in case there was a briefcase under a lounge chair. But ladies with shoestrings between their buns apparently didn't carry briefcases.

He reached the end, reversed himself, and paddled back. A pool like this, he observed, could be improved by putting a few salmon in it.

He emerged and shook himself vigorously, sending a halo of water around himself. Then he walked off with his robe draped over his arm. He went up a few tiled stairs, past a lighted bubbling fountain on which petals floated. The path opened into a small courtyard with more animal-headed fountains, and his room faced all this splendor. His doorway was framed by flowering plants and trees, their rich scent playing in his nostrils as he passed them. A bee flew out of a blossom, and he caught it and ate it, then looked around nervously.

I really shouldn't be eating hotel property, he told himself. But the old habits die hard.

He entered his room. It was large and cool, with double doors at the other end, leading to a private garden protected by a high redwood fence. He ordered some breakfast for himself and the guest he was expecting, then waited in his garden in a white lounge chair beneath a tree. He was wearing sunglasses, and his white bathrobe bore the hotel monogram—a swan.

He peeled a piece of bark off the tree and nibbled on its rich interior. The vegetation in Southern California was heavy with juice. That, and the fact that women wore shoelaces between their buns, were strong points in favor of permanently denning here.

A waiter arrived with a serving table on which a breakfast was laid for two. A jar of special honey had been provided, with macadamia nuts floating in it. Beside it lay a folded copy of the *Los Angeles Times*.

"Will there be anything else, sir?" asked the waiter.

"No, that's all," said the bear, and signed the bill in his slow, careful style.

When the waiter left, the bear opened the paper and checked the best-seller list. *Destiny and Desire* was still number one.

There was a knock at the door. He opened it for his Hollywood agent.

"Hi," said Zou Zou Sharr hesitantly, not knowing how things stood between them any longer.

"Come on in," said the bear genially.

Zou Zou's outfit—a simple tailored suit—reflected her uncertainty. She didn't want it to seem as if she were presenting herself as a physical object. He showed her out to the garden, and when she saw the jar of honey, a twinge of melancholy went through her for those first days in New York, before the whirlwind had swept him away to stardom. She laid the tip of her red fingernail on the best-seller page. "You must be very happy."

He bit into a ten-dollar slice of papaya. "Do you wear a shoelace between your buns?"

"On occasion," she said nervously. He was the New Presence. He was hot. The A-list actresses were after him. How could she compete? But did the A-list actresses understand him?

"Success has been easy for you, hasn't it, Hal?" she suggested hopefully.

"Signing my name is tough."

"What do you mean?" Her emotional antenna folded back down and her business antenna went up. True, he'd signed with her agency, but agreements were made to be broken. Had CAA swept in to grab him? "You're not going to do better with another agency, Hal, no matter who may be sweet-talking you."

"If I don't hold the pen right I make a mess."

"What kind of a mess?" Her antenna was humming now. CAA *had* moved in, the predatory bastards, and Hal was telling her if he didn't get what he wanted there was going to be a costly contractual battle. God, he's such a shrewd negotiator, able to unnerve you with just a few words. "What do you want, Hal? Tell me now before things get ugly. Has CAA offered you a house out here? We'll get you a better one. With a car, a driver, whatever you want. But we *have* to have your next book."

"I haven't been able to find it."

She saw he was going to stonewall them. There'd be no new book without a new contract. "What have they offered you that we can't get you too? Whatever you want, Hal, it's yours. We'll give you a house, a car, and a maid wearing a shoelace between her buns." Zou Zou stood, smoothing down the front of her skirt. Any silly romantic notion she'd had when she'd walked in was buried now. She believed in enduring love, but what truly endured was money. "You and I can drive around and look at real estate. We'd all love to help you settle out here." She closed her eyes. "I can just see you in Topanga Canyon."

The telephone rang. The bear cradled it to his ear. "Yes?"

"Hal, this is Elliot. There's a little problem here in New York."

"Problem?"

"Some nut is suing you. He claims you stole his book."

The bear dropped the phone into its cradle. He looked at Zou Zou Sharr, but hardly recognized her.

"Hal, what is it?"

He got up abruptly from the table and looked at the redwood fence.

Now, said an ancient voice. *While you've got the chance. Run!*

Primal landscapes flashed past his mind's eye. He slapped violently at the trunk of the tree, to make loud sounds that would frighten his enemies. Then he grabbed the tree and shook it so violently its roots bulged up from the ground. Zou Zou was only mildly terrified, having seen him in this mood the very first day they'd met. She put out her hand to him. "Hal, it's me, Zou Zou."

"Zoo?"

"Zou Zou."

He swung around, his lips parting in a snarl, and she backed up immediately.

240

He spied the jar of honey on the table, with macadamias suspended in the golden hue, and he groaned with anguish. My life as a human being, my honey and sunglasses—he groaned again—it's going to be taken from me.

He leapt toward the table, opened the honey, and drained it down while it was still available. His thoughts went no further than that, the moment was all he had, with its fragments of desires and fears. He started gobbling up the rest of the two breakfasts.

Over the fence! said the ancient voice. *Follow your nose to freedom!*

"Hal," said Zou Zou, "you can confide in me."

He looked at her with uncomprehending eyes. What did this female want? Was she connected to the zoo? He let out a roar and tipped over the table.

Zou Zou leapt away. "I've caught you at a bad time, Hal. I'll call later." She was picking papaya rind off her skirt as she backed up. Her client was clearly out of his mind for the moment, which *can* be a good time to renegotiate. A plateful of eggs came at her through the air. "Call the agency, Hal, we'll get you anything you want." She ducked into the hallway and closed the door behind her as another plate struck the wall.

The bear raged around in his private garden, shaking the tree and the fence. Then he bent the iron garden furniture.

There's no time for that, said the voice. *Run for your life!*

The bear took a last look around at the luxury he must leave behind. He was going to miss feathery pillows and room service. He'd miss lounging around at poolside. He'd miss women's shiny buns. He picked up the *Los Angeles Times* from the ground, wanting a last look at his name on the best-seller list, but before he found it an advertisement caught his eye.

TITLE FOR SALE

What's this? wondered the bear. Was it possible he could *buy* his new book? Elliot was always after him for the next title, and here was one for sale. It might solve his current problem of being sued. A second book would make everybody forget about the first one, which he'd stolen. He read the first line of the advertisement.

FOR IMMEDIATE SALE—A DISTINGUISHED BRITISH TITLE.

Nothing wrong with that, thought the bear. A title is a title.

THIS RARE OPPORTUNITY BECOMES AVAILABLE WHEN A PREVIOUS TITLEHOLDER WISHES TO TRANSFER OWNERSHIP. ONLY A

SMALL NUMBER OF TITLES ARE EVER OFFERED IN THIS WAY, AND IT IS SELDOM THAT THEY REMAIN ON THE MARKET FOR LONG.

Fine, thought the bear. The previous owner is selling the title. I don't have to steal it. I buy it.

THE PRIVILEGES THAT GO WITH TITLE ARE MANY. ELEVATED SOCIAL STATUS, PRESTIGE, AND THE ESTEEM CONNECTED TO AN OLD TITLE—AND *THIS* TITLE IS VERY OLD—CANNOT BE EASILY CALCULATED.

That's what I want, thought the bear. Elevated social status, so I can't be put in a zoo.

A TITLE WILL OPEN DOORS THAT ARE CLOSED TO ALL *BUT* THE TITLED, AND FROM THIS ENHANCED POSITION ADVANTAGEOUS RELATIONSHIPS WILL BE FORMED BOTH SOCIALLY AND PROFESSIONALLY. THE PRICE FOR THE FULLY DOCUMENTED TITLE— LORD OF OVERLOOK IN THE COUNTY OF DEVON—IS US$35,000.

The bear set the paper down and called London immediately.
"*Bagget and Smallwood.*"
"I need to buy a title."
"*One moment, please, I'll connect you.*" There was a

pause and then a man came on the line. *"Bagget here. How may I help you?"*

"I want to buy a title," said the bear.

"Very good, sir. And you are—?"

"Hal Jam."

"Calling from?"

"Los Angeles."

"Yes of course, sir, I see." The mention of Los Angeles put a lift into Bagget's response, for he received many crank inquiries, but Los Angeles was a likely place to sell an English title, of that Bagget had no doubt, and it was for this reason he'd advertised there.

"A bear can own the title, can't he?" asked the bear nervously.

Bagget pressed the receiver to his ear, thinking there was something wrong with the connection. He winged an answer. *"Most of the newer title acquisitions are made by citizens of other countries."*

"Good," said the bear.

"The title is a very old and fine one, Mr. Jam," said Bagget. *"The pedigree is handsome and without flaws. The first Lord Overlook was granted his title by King Edward the Elder in 923, so you can see we are discussing a hallowed title indeed."*

"That's what the title is? *Lord Overlook?*"

"Yes."

The bear probed with his paw in the empty honey

jar. *Lord Overlook* sounded like a historical novel dealing with kings. Kings were dominant males so it should make for lively reading. "Okay, I'll buy it."

"Acquisition of the title is only a matter of you transferring $35,000 in U.S. funds to our bank here, which is Barclays of London."

"How soon do I get the title?"

"Five days should see it in your hands, Lord Overlook," said Bagget, now keenly aware that he had a live fish on the line.

"I'll send the money right away," said the bear.

"Very good, Lord Overlook. Very good indeed. All the paperwork will be forwarded immediately. It will include your various rights and the complete historical documentation."

"What rights?"

"There are fishing rights in the streams of Overlook, which I'm told are well stocked."

"I love to fish," said the bear, salivating.

"There are possible mineral rights too, though nothing of substantial value has been found in the ground there for several centuries, but it never hurts to look, eh?"

"That's right," said the bear. "Squirrels hide things."

Bagget faltered momentarily. The man sounded like a simpleton. Mental defectives sometimes placed calls such as this. *"You say you're at—?"*

"The Bel Air hotel. I'm an author."

Bagget's confidence was renewed, as he classed

245

American writers beside Russian gangsters, with whom he had done some title business in the past. Gangsters found a title helpful when they were arrested. *"You may put your title on your passport, checkbooks, and credit cards, a nice advantage, Lord Overlook. Imagine the impression you will make at a hotel when you pass across a credit card bearing your title."*

"That's what I need to make," said the bear. "An impression."

"I quite understand. Along those same lines, you can expect to have your application for membership to the most exclusive clubs in the world greatly expedited. And you shall undoubtedly be invited to functions at which royalty will be present."

"Princess Diana?"

"Very possibly."

"She has nice buns."

"I share some of your feeling, sir," said Bagget, and pressed forward to safer ground. *"I should alert you—you may also find yourself being offered appointments to company boards. I have no doubt there are many companies in the Los Angeles area who would be honored to have you on their board."*

"How about if I'm being sued?"

"I sincerely hope you are not, but should that be the case, the prestige of a legitimate title will weigh heavily in your favor with any court in the civilized world. I suggest we con-

clude our business directly, so the protection your title affords will become operative at once. For that, as I said, we need only your funds wired to our bank."

"No problem," said the bear.

"I should tell you that no land comes with the title, but if you wish to purchase a home in North Devon, where Overlook is situated, Bagget and Smallwood stand ready to serve you in this way. Overlook is lovely farm country, and I'm sure we could find you a few acres with a substantial dwelling attached. You could walk on the very land that has been part of your title's glorious history."

The bear returned to New York City as Overlook, Twenty-fifth Lord of the Manor, North Devon. Elliot Gadson assured him that there was nothing to worry about as regards the lawsuit. Not only was the legal staff of Cavendish Press already at work, but the legal eagles of the parent company, Tempo Oil, were also on the job, ". . . and those boys hit hard, Hal. They don't want their best-selling author troubled."

The bear understood by now that he'd purchased not a book title but a form of identity, which was even better. He'd instructed Bagget and Smallwood to buy him a stately home in Overlook, so he would soon have a manor to be lord of. Bagget and Smallwood had sent him a plaque bearing the Overlook coat of arms, and it was displayed on his living room wall. He thought such a display was classy. This was because he was a bear.

He stretched out on his living room rug, on top of an electronic massage mat which directed small motorized rollers and fingers into various parts of his back, scratching where he couldn't reach. Laying his paws together on his stomach as the rollers ran up his spine, he thought about how he used to have to do this sort of thing himself against a tree trunk—how crude, how primitive. His tongue slipped slowly outward at the corner of his mouth and hung there ecstatically.

His ecstasy was interrupted by the door buzzer. With a sigh, he switched off the scratcher and went toward the door. Building security sent no one up without announcing them, so the bear assumed the man who greeted him on the other side of the door was from the maintenance crew. "Do you need to fix something?" asked the bear.

"Are you Hal Jam?"

"Sure."

The man extended a folded sheet of paper. "I'm serving you with this."

"Thank you," said the bear. He liked being served. He gave the man a ten-dollar tip.

The man looked at the ten-dollar bill regretfully. "Sorry, I can't take it." The man walked back toward the elevator and the bear retired into his apartment. Elliot Gadson had told him he was probably going to win something called the National Book Award. Was this it? He unfolded the paper the man had given him. The words were nice and big, the way he liked them. He read slowly:

SUPERIOR COURT
AROOSTOOK COUNTY, MAINE

SUMMONS IN A CIVIL ACTION

ARTHUR BRAMHALL

v.

THE CAVENDISH PRESS
AND HAL JAM, A PERSON
PRETENDING TO BE THE AUTHOR OF
DESTINY AND DESIRE

Was this the National Book Award? The bear turned the paper in his paws as if changing the angle would help him understand it better. Then he sniffed it. There was only the flat scent of paper and the pungent imprint of the thumb of the man who'd brought it; it smelled like pastrami; much as the bear liked this smell, he somehow sensed it wasn't relevant. And slowly, very slowly, he began to grasp the significance of the piece of paper.

He stared at the summons as if teeth of steel were buried under its surface. He could fight a pack of hungry wild dogs but how could he fight a piece of paper? The trap had sprung and had him in its jaws.

He threw the summons to the floor. "I'll pretend it never came," he said aloud, but even as he said it he knew that this wouldn't work.

The summons lay almost smugly, as if it knew it held him in a grip from which he couldn't escape. He stared at the white, rectangular shape. He could pounce on it, rip it to shreds, and swallow the pieces, but its sinister power would be undiminished.

He sank heavily into his beanbag chair and reached for his honey jar. He opened it, drained it desperately, wanting oblivion, wanting to float away on a sea of sweetness. He wiped his mouth with the back of his paw.

The dreadful summons lay near his toe. He touched it lightly, expecting it to hiss or possibly even speak, to say, *"You will be caged tomorrow."*

He laid his heel on it and dragged it toward his chair. Recklessly, the way he tore into hives for honey, he grabbed the summons and shook it, hoping the words would fly off the paper like bees. But no bright winged little bombers attacked him. The hive of words was indifferent to his attack.

The bear read the summons again slowly, moving his paw along under the words. He read the entire summons over several times:

ARTHUR BRAMHALL

v.

THE CAVENDISH PRESS

AND HAL JAM, A PERSON . . .

He let out a roar of delight and threw the summons in the air.

"A person! They called me a person!" He retrieved the paper from the floor and read it aloud: *"Hal Jam, a person."* No mistake about it.

He carried the summons over to his desk and laid it carefully down. This was the most important document he'd ever received. "A *person* . . . not a bear. I've done it. I'm a person. It's official."

He danced around on the carpet, paws in the air. "I'm finally a member of the human race!"

"Come in, my lord, come in." Elliot Gadson was waiting in a conference room at Cavendish Press, along with a lawyer from Tempo Oil, who showed the sort of deference toward title that Bagget and Smallwood had predicted in their ad. The bear entered with a light step, since he was not only a Lord of the Manor but more important, a person. He took a seat at the head of the table. The lawyer, observing his self-possession, put it down not just to his aristocratic lineage but to the innocence of a writer having nothing to fear from a crank with a nuisance suit. Gadson, who had a flair for dramatic formality, was delighted to be able to make the sort of introduction now required. "Hal Jam, twenty-fifth Lord of Overlook."

"John Warwick," said Tempo Oil's senior attorney.

Warwick's face expressed experience gained in matters of great complexity, involving billions of oily dollars. He knew how to take stock of a man quickly and he was pleased with Jam's appearance. His air of robust strength, confidence, and good health would play well in court. "I'm sorry we have to bother you at all with this business, but it shouldn't take long for us to put things right. I thought your book was a real page-turner, and so did my wife."

The bear nodded his thanks, that of a judicially certified person.

"You're important to us, Hal." Warwick gestured toward Gadson, who made a small, appropriate sound in response. "It's no secret we're in business to make money," continued Warwick. "And it's also no secret that you've made a lot of it for us. We're here to protect you and ourselves. Now—" He opened his briefcase and placed some papers on the desk. "We've received interrogatories you'll need to answer. They've been sent to us by the lawyer representing the individual who's brought the suit against you." Warwick handed the papers to Jam. "It's just straightforward stuff. Place and date of birth, and so on."

The bear stared down at the questions. He'd been born in a hollow tree trunk. His previous address was a cave. He looked back up at Warwick. "No." He handed the interrogatories back.

"I know they're trivial questions, Hal, and they're certainly a waste of your time and ours. But that's what this whole suit is, you see. It's meant to be troublesome and costly so that we'll capitulate and settle. But we aren't going to do that."

"It's not that I'm not a person," explained the bear. "I'm definitely a person."

Gadson intervened, feeling the point was a delicate one and that he was more sensitive to it than others might be. "Hal is very careful about his background. We've had a close professional relationship, and yet he never once mentioned that he was an English lord. I raise this point to show how private a person he really is. Most people in this day and age couldn't wait to trot out their pedigree, if they had one. But Hal, to his great credit, feels it's inappropriate that he should have to speak of his background. Am I correct in this, Hal?"

"I'm a person. It says so right here." The bear waved the summons at Warwick.

Warwick was used to fighting environmentalists and had been looking at this Jam action as a welcome change—nobody'd spilled oil on anyone's duck. But Jam was . . . well . . . strange. Warwick was aware that English aristocrats could be that way. He cleared his throat and tried again: "What it says on that summons, Hal, is that somebody claiming to be you is suing you for claiming to be him. It's a bogus claim, since you're an estab-

lished author, and a lord, and he's an opportunist, or—
and this is a real possibility in this kind of case—he's
deluded. Either way, we need your response to these interrogatories. We need to establish your bona fides." Warwick smiled the patient smile he used when a Tempo Oil
tanker was sinking in offshore waters. "I understand that
you feel it unnecessary to talk about your illustrious family. And I'm also aware that you've cultivated a mystique
of mystery to help sell your book. We're not going to
disturb that mystique. In fact, we're going to preserve and
enhance it. But what we're preserving first and foremost is
your money. And ours." He slid the interrogatories along
the edge of the conference table toward Jam.

The bear pushed them back. "No."

"But why, Hal? I mean, my lord? What objection do
you have to telling us when and where you were born?
We're not going to publish it."

Again Gadson intervened. "Hal's life is his writer's
capital. He doesn't wish to draw from it unnecessarily."

"He'll be drawing from his capital big-time if we lose
this case."

"He's refused to answer our interrogatories," said Eaton Magoon. "I've no idea why. He has Tempo Oil attorneys representing him, so I assume they're up to something dirty. I'm going to make a motion to compel." Magoon had the reputation of being a shrewd old-fashioned country lawyer, with plenty of horse sense. "By the way, Bramhall, have you got another suit of clothes? That one doesn't fit you."

"It used to fit."

"When, in high school? The sleeves are nearly up to your elbows. The waistband is split."

An impatient growl escaped Bramhall's lips, for it cost him a great deal to be here at all. Shadows from the cave still disturbed his perception. Objects in Magoon's office that should have been familiar—a clock, a picture frame, a file folder—appeared sinister, pieces of a grand delusion he must now rejoin. Only the breeze coming in at the window seemed companionable. His feet felt horribly cramped in the shoes he wore; he longed to walk barefoot over the pine-needled floor of a forest lit by the soft moon of dreams. These memories clung to him, discreetly agitating their case, while Magoon explained the other case, the real one, and what they needed to do to win it. "I suggest you buy a suit that fits you. A man whose jacket rides up to the elbow and whose pants are split does not make a good impression on a jury."

Again, Bramhall snarled a reply. He was irascible, the way bears are in springtime, and it worried him, because he felt capable of seriously injuring someone, anyone, who got in his way. His emotions were hardly recognizable to him. At some moments he felt like an authority, a king. And this would be followed just as quickly by a feeling of numbing stupidity, in which his thoughts wouldn't move at all. Other times he felt like his old self, a lonely university professor, socially inept but hardworking and clever, clever enough to have written a best-seller. And then a bear's blind rage would surface.

Magoon saw the confusion in his client's eyes and leaned forward in a kindly manner, his fingers intertwined. "I'm beginning to think we have a case. It's possible they didn't answer our interrogatories because there's something in the man's past that's shady. I don't dare count on that, but I can hope for it. And I hope for something else, Bramhall. May I continue to speak frankly?"

257

Bramhall shrugged his assent. Magoon said, "I hope that you can, between now and the trial, learn to speak more clearly."

Bramhall groaned. "I've developed . . . an impediment."

"Speech impediments can sometimes win a jury's sympathy." Magoon rocked back in his chair and laid his intertwined fingers on his paunch. "But you sound as if you're tearing your way through a hunk of raw meat. I don't think a jury will find it a sympathetic sound."

"I know," growled Bramhall. "It's terrible."

"A speech therapist might be able to help you."

"I used to speak perfectly well."

"And your suit used to fit." Magoon turned toward the window and gazed out thoughtfully toward the fading logo of the Feed and Seed store. "Maybe I should tell the court you received a throat injury playing football. Or while rescuing a drowning child. Yes, that's better." He turned back to Bramhall. "The rescue ropes twisted, and caught you in the larynx."

"My voice changed while I was sleeping in a cave."

"Again—not the sort of thing a jury would find sympathetic. But just for my own enlightenment, why were you sleeping in a cave?"

"I was demoralized. I wanted to live like an animal."

"And?"

"I felt . . . drawn to a cave. I spent most of the winter there."

"You spent the Maine winter in a cave?" Magoon stared hard into Bramhall's eyes, trying to judge his client's mental condition. Bramhall's gaze was tortured but Magoon could discern no true signs of lunacy. "You need a haircut, a shave, and a new suit. Will you take care of those things?"

"Yes."

"Good."

Bramhall ran a hand over the thick stubble that covered his face. "I have to shave three times a day now." He ran a hand over his forehead. "And I've gotten hairy. The mind . . . can affect the body."

"I suggest a depilatory cream."

"Whatever you say."

"The little details, Bramhall. They could be important." Magoon's nose wrinkled. "And strong cologne. I think a good daub of that wouldn't hurt either."

Bramhall lowered his head sideways, sniffing. "I know, I smell like an animal."

"Perhaps *several* good daubs of strong cologne. Better yet, splash it all over yourself."

"All right," said Bramhall with the chastised look of a bad dog.

"I don't want to tell you what to do. But we need to

present you in the most favorable light we can. When you pass the jury box, I want them to see an upstanding member of the community. Someone with whom they feel they have something in common."

"I've gotten very shy of people."

"Shy is fine, it can be an endearing quality. But you look *hunted*. All the time you've been sitting here, you've been glancing back over your shoulder."

"I *feel* hunted."

"You're in my office. No one's threatening you. If they do, I'll have them arrested." Magoon looked back down at his notes and gave himself over to reflection. He had a shot at winning this case because Bramhall was telling the truth.

Magoon swiveled toward the window while imagining his approach to the jury. *My client has been robbed of his most valuable possession. He's been driven nearly insane by the loss.*

He looked back at Bramhall's tormented face. The suffering look could help, as long as his suit fit.

"The court has compelled us to answer," said Warwick.

"Hal won't agree to it," said Gadson.

"He has no choice."

"He's such a private person. Perhaps if you filled out the interrogatories yourself and just handed them to him for signature—"

"Are you asking a lawyer of my stature to fabricate facts for a client?"

"Well, how about if Bettina fabricates the facts? She's already made up all kinds of stories about him. She could just finish the job."

"There you are, Hal," said Bettina. "All you have to do is sign them."

The bear looked at the interrogatories suspiciously.

Bettina laid her hand gently on his shoulder. "Don't worry, Hal. It looks very official, but it's just another kind of publicity. These are only little details about your life that people will enjoy reading."

The bear sniffed the interrogatories. They were laden with Bettina's perfume, which reassured him. He read them over, moving his paw along very slowly under each line. They described a real person, with a place and date of birth, and a lot of other swell things. He began to feel very good about the interrogatories. In fact, he was proud of them. They were *his* interrogatories. "Mine," he said, and signed.

It was springtime when the bear's case came up before the superior court in Maine. He and his lawyer, John Warwick, checked into the only lodging available in town—a dilapidated bed-and-breakfast on Main Street. The front porch held a semicircle of rickety rocking chairs, in which they now sat. To one side of them was the volunteer firehouse and on the other a live-bait shop. Murmuring somewhere in back was the river which had given the town its feeble reason to exist.

"Well, it's certainly a change," said Warwick as a wreath of black flies circled his head.

The bear sniffed the air. A spring rain cloud was overhead, ready to drench the surrounding forest. Its hovering presence troubled him, for it was a distiller of many familiar scents, gathered from the forest's floor. The songs of the birds were colored by the moist, heavy air, and he resented their anticipation of the storm; they celebrated what he could not, for he no longer walked in the rain. He had an umbrella now, for emergencies.

"I always say I'll rent a place in the country for the summer. But I never do." Warwick's voice had a melancholy tone, of a busy man used to denying himself what he longed for. "Something always comes up. That's the way, isn't it?"

"Yes," said the bear, wondering why his beloved forest wasn't his anymore. Then he remembered and said aloud, "I'm a person."

Warwick glanced at him. Jam certainly said some odd things. Warwick had a large and thoroughgoing staff, and he knew by now that Jam had bought his title. Warwick's staff had also summarized for him all the major plagiary cases of the past fifty years. They'd built a dossier on the plaintiff, Arthur Bramhall, which went back to the day of his birth. But they'd been unable to find anything at all on the life of their own client, Hal Jam. Warwick was disturbed by Jam's lack of cooperation, and even more deeply disturbed by the fact that the man had no past. In this life, everyone has a past, unless he has deliberately destroyed all traces of it.

The bear rocked in his chair, nose sifting and sorting the elements of springtime in his home territory. The moist air brought the smell of wild animals going their solitary ways—a deer nibbling new buds, a fox stalking on tiptoe, a porcupine slowly climbing a tree. His blood stirred with the old magic, and his rocker began to creak more rapidly. I could slip away. In a minute I'd be gone. This mess I'm in would hang behind me like an empty spider's web, to which no one ever returns. The valleys, the meadows, honey in the comb would be mine again. I'd stamp the earth, I'd shake the mountain with my roar.

He sprang from the rocker, his primal self waking from its hibernation in the plush velvet cave of man. He filled his lungs with the impending storm and shook his head with short, sharp snaps to clear it of the last silky, sticky threads of detestable indulgence.

A dented airport taxi pulled in beside the bed-and-breakfast. "Hal, I'm so relieved to see you," said Chum Boykins, hurrying up the porch steps, suitcase in hand. "I got away as soon as I could. Here, I brought us a New York City cheesecake, as an aid to concentration."

The bear's spirit faltered, the smell of the cheesecake obliterating other smells as he lowered his nose toward its moist, sweet, fascinating surface.

Boykins turned to Warwick. "How do things look?"

"Fine," said Warwick, his confident veneer what one would expect from a man who could put on a good face while 200,000 barrels of oil were being spilled into prime fishing waters.

Boykins sat down, his fevered gaze falling on two empty rockers beside him. He made a few corrective touches to their positioning. "Bettina said she can put a positive spin on the lawsuit story, that it's just more publicity for Hal, but I don't like it at all. Any hint of plagiary is deadly. Reputations can be spoiled overnight." Boykins made a further adjustment on one of the empty rockers, making it nice and straight for Mickey Mouse, should the rodent drop by. As the day of the lawsuit had drawn near, his doctor had had to switch him from Prozac to Zoloft. He shifted his gaze toward the dark wooded hills that ringed the town. "I guess all this uncharted wilderness must really inspire the hell out of you, Hal. But how you turned such a godforsaken place into such an inspiring story is amazing, really. Because there's nothing here. You look at it, and what is it? Trees, hills, a skunk, a two-by-nothing town. Is the next book going to take place around here too?"

"I haven't found it yet," said the bear, mouth stuffed with cheesecake.

"My instinct says go with what worked last time."

"Maybe I'll never find it."

"Don't say that, Hal. Book number two is already shaping itself inside you." Boykins cared deeply about his author's future. Agents came and went, compulsive agents came and went several times, but there was only one Hal Jam. And Boykins felt there was disaster ahead for him.

"Why am I bothering with it, Vinal?" It was night, and Bramhall was seated with Pinette in front of the old lumberjack's kitchen stove. The kitchen was lit by a single bare bulb hanging from the ceiling, and moths were fluttering against the window screen, trying to reach the light that had lured them from the fields. "Why am I fighting this battle?"

"To find out what happened to your suitcase. My guess is, this feller Jam musta shot the bear while the bear was lugging the suitcase around. Jam reads the book, says well it ain't much use to the bear any longer, then takes off with it." Pinette poked at the fire in his kitchen stove. "The question in my mind is, did he boil the bear down? Because you hate to see lovely grease like that go to waste."

Bramhall turned to the window. A huge luna moth had flown against the screen, its pale green wings working furiously.

"By god," said Pinette, "that's a big feller. You don't see him too often."

Bramhall stared at the great moth and felt a fragile emotion flit through him. He'd turned his back on the forest, but it had not forgotten him; this green-cloaked messenger of the night had sought him out, to remind him of those enchanted regions he'd explored both awake and in his dreams. The eyes of the moth were glittering; its huge antennae waved, and its wings moved so quickly they created a mesmerizing luminosity. Bramhall abruptly rose and went into Pinette's living room. The bulky, misshapen cushions of its couch and armchairs were sunk in shadows, and Bramhall stood there in the gloom until the enchantment passed, and he felt as dull and misshapen as the furniture.

After supper at the local diner, the bear, his lawyer, and his agent strolled along Main Street. Boykins gazed downward as he walked, to avoid the cracks in the sidewalk.

"Look for a briefcase," said the bear.

"Why, did you lose one?"

"Somebody might have," said the bear.

John Warwick had been listening in silence to the conversation of the two men as they walked. Jam had tremendous presence, but what he said made little sense. What the hell kind of defendant would he be?

Boykins continued counting the cracks.

What's going on here? the bear asked himself as he sniffed Arthur Bramhall's scent across the courtroom. He turned to his lawyer and said, "He's a bear."

"What?"

"A bear!" said the bear excitedly. "He's a bear who's trying to become a person!"

Some members of the jury had turned to look at them, and Warwick said softly, "We'll talk later, Hal."

Chum Boykins entered the courtroom. He went through a brief ritual of sitting in several different seats before finally choosing the one that felt indisputably right. Then he got up and chose another one.

Eaton Magoon, at the plaintiff's table, looked like the proverbial cracker-barrel rube, wearing a plaid shirt and wide suspenders with his suit. Alongside Magoon sat Arthur Bramhall in a new suit from J. C. Penney. It didn't fit much better than his other suits, as he'd been bewildered when he'd purchased it. Before coming to the courtroom, he'd emptied a bottle of Brut cologne on himself, but he knew he still smelled like an animal. His head was down, as he could not yet bring himself to face this human gathering. Depressed, alienated, with hair on his forehead, he surreptitiously lifted his eyes as his lawyer stepped forward to make the opening statement to the court:

"Your honor, ladies and gentlemen, Arthur Bramhall worked at his craft daily, in a small cabin some of you might know if you've done any hunting around here. Arthur is happy to let folks hunt through his land because it gives him pleasure to look up from his work and see a neighbor moving across the old field, on the lookout for small game. Arthur's own game is different, however. Arthur hunts words, trying to bag the perfect phrase. Anyone who comes down his lane knows what they'll see— Arthur at his window, hunched over his typewriter, re-creating life as he knows it, life in Maine, the way life should be." Magoon gave the jury a neighborly smile. "At first, he was *from away*. But he quickly adjusted. He learned what country life is all about and he respected it and finally he was able to write about it, as if he'd always lived here."

Magoon paused and let his gaze move slowly from one juror to the other. "And after writing about our life here, after devoting his entire sabbatical to writing about life here in Maine, his book was stolen from him."

Magoon walked back and forth, gesturing dramatically, and the bear watched him closely, trying to imagine himself walking back and forth like that, saying complicated things and punctuating his remarks with forceful paw movements.

"My client has been driven nearly insane by the loss of his manuscript, over which he struggled so desperately for so long. Look at him, ladies and gentlemen of the jury, and see the suffering in his face. That is the face of a man whose life's work has been stolen from him. He was once a college professor. Yes, right here at our own University of Maine. He's lost that job, friends. He cannot hold a teaching post any longer, because he can hardly speak. His voice has been affected by his loss, as has his overall appearance. He's so wretched, my friends, *his bodily functions have been altered.*"

The bear nodded approvingly, taking pleasure from the rhythmic flow of Magoon's incomprehensible words. It was like the babbling of a Maine stream in springtime.

"Hal," hissed John Warwick, *"stop nodding."* Warwick was growing more concerned. His adversary, Magoon, was a first-rate ham playing to a hometown jury. And Judge Wendell Spurr looked like he might resent a big-city lawyer with a celebrity client. Especially a client who was nodding as if he agreed with Magoon's accusations against him.

Warwick cast a sidelong glance at the celebrated novelist and wondered: What the hell is wrong with Jam anyway? He doesn't seem to care what's happening here.

". . . and we'll prove, ladies and gentlemen, beyond any doubt, that my client wrote *Destiny and Desire* and that this person—" Magoon pointed at the bear. The bear nodded enthusiastically at being called a person and drummed his paws together.

"—*this* person, who seems to have no conscience whatsoever, stole *Destiny and Desire,* pawned it off as his own, and profited enormously. Profited through the fruits of my client's labors, profited through another man's inspiration. That's not how we do things here in Maine. And yet this person now sits smugly satisfied in this courtroom, believing himself above the law." Magoon directed a withering look at the bear, who returned it with a friendly wave, which threw Magoon for a loop.

What does he have up his sleeve? wondered Magoon. What kind of strategy has Warwick given him? Magoon looked at the power attorney's steel-gray hair, his calculating eyes, his Rolex watch. And his client was acting like a man who knew he couldn't lose. Jesus, thought Magoon, I've gotten in over my head. He shot a sidelong glance at Arthur Bramhall, who didn't have a penny to his name, for whom he was working on contingency and to whom he'd already committed large blocks of time.

Warwick stood before the jury and made his opening statement, defending his client against "this ludicrous accusation. Hal Jam is known across the country for his brilliance, his philosophic wit, his sense of humor, all the things, in short, that we'd expect from the man who wrote *Destiny and Desire.*"

Warwick cast a glance toward Arthur Bramhall and the jury followed his gaze, their eye falling on the man who looked like a lumberjack at a funeral. As he felt the eyes of the jury on him, Bramhall lowered his head still further, the expression on his face that of an animal who'd been caught at some piece of mischief, like a raccoon stealing eggs from a henhouse.

"My client," continued Warwick, bringing his gaze back to the impeccably attired bear, "is a man of spotless reputation who has achieved a high position in the literary world. On his recent book tour, he saved the life of the vice president of the United States, an act of incredible heroism I'm sure many of you may recall. He is a man of culture and breeding. He is—and this is a little-known fact—a titled lord." Warwick paused and made a slight bow toward the bear. "He is Lord Overlook, of North Devon, England."

Eaton Magoon was on his feet. "Objection, your honor!"

Judge Wendell Spurr jerked his head up from the half-slumber he usually indulged in at court, and adjusted his robe. A lord, thought Judge Spurr. My, my, let's sit up and do things right. An image of white-wigged English barristers and magistrates floated through his mind and he felt himself suddenly linked to a great tradition. He shot an unsympathetic look at Magoon. The astonishing revelation that he had an English lord in his court had given Judge Spurr a welcome lift, and he wasn't going to let the likes of Eaton Magoon spoil it. Along with the image of wigged judges, he now had an image of shooting partridge on the Overlook estate; he could see himself walking across an English field, gun in hand, Lord Overlook by his side. He scowled toward the plaintiff's bench. "What's your problem, Mr. Magoon?"

"This information isn't relevant to the case, your honor," said Magoon, attempting to paddle upstream. A single glance at the jury showed him how impressed they were. And so was he.

"I'm overruling you," said Judge Spurr. "The background of both parties is relevant."

Magoon sat down, and Warwick continued. "Lord Overlook does not use his title ordinarily, for he's a modest man. It doesn't appear on his books or in any publicity connected to his name. But you'll find it in the great book of British history, at the Royal Commission of Manuscripts, and in the Local Public Records Office of North Devon. It is a title that has descended to him from a family that goes back a thousand years to the time of King Edward, when the Overlook family first swore their allegiance to the crown." Again Warwick gave a slight bow of his head, as if the crown floated in the air before them like the Grail. He was pleased to see that several members of the jury had bowed their heads too.

"He is a man who has no need to steal another man's book, for fame or glory. He has fame enough, ladies and gentlemen of the jury, and a fine, old, hallowed name, a name that means respectability and power. A lord of the English realm does not need to come to this peaceful town in Maine and appropriate an identity. He has an enviable identity already. It is far more likely that someone would try to appropriate *his* identity." Warwick gestured toward his adversary's table and then abruptly sat down.

Magoon rose again, shaking his head and giving a neighborly smile to the jury, as if he and they had just listened to an aluminum-siding salesman. But he was greatly disturbed by this English lord thing. The jury was still looking at Warwick's client with eager curiosity. The only genuine glamour in their lives until now had been Dollar-Daze up at the shopping mall, wet T-shirt night at the Chain Saw bar, and angel books written by Eunice Cotton which they purchased at the convenience store. Into this innocent rural setting had strode someone called Lord Overlook of North Devon.

Magoon called his first witness, the old lumberjack Vinal Pinette. Magoon hoped he'd win some jury sympathy with a man they all knew, whose backwoods style rang with honesty.

"Mr. Pinette," said Magoon, "do you recognize that

man over there? Is he someone with whom you are familiar?"

Pinette looked at his friend. "He's my neighbor, Art Bramhall."

"Could you tell the court what sort of man he is?"

"Pretty good feller."

"Do you visit him often?"

"Yessir, we do a bit of jawing."

"And when you go to visit him, what do you usually find him doing?"

"Setting in the hog trough."

The jury let out a snicker and Eaton Magoon rushed to correct the impression. "You find him in the hog trough now that he's been demoralized, now that he has fallen into depression over the loss of his book, now that he has almost lost the will to live. But previous to that, you used to find him at work at his desk writing, didn't you?"

Warwick came to his feet. "Objection, your honor. He's leading the witness."

"Sustained."

"Forgive me, your honor. Mr. Pinette, did you ever see Arthur Bramhall in the act of writing?"

"I been giving him some pretty fair ideas. He ain't had a chance to write 'em up yet."

"But you know he's a writer?"

"Yep."

"You've seen his typewriter?"

"Once or twice."

"And his house is filled with books?"

"Smartest thing he ever done was line his walls with books. Books is better than wood shavings any day when it comes to insulating a house." Pinette looked at the jury and prepared to embark upon a discussion of insulating materials for houses, but Magoon brought him back to the matter at hand.

"Mr. Bramhall doesn't have books for insulation. He has books because he reads them. Isn't that right?"

"Maybe so," said Pinette, reluctant to commit too quickly to such a radical notion as someone reading as many books as Art Bramhall had.

"And the reason he reads them is because he's a writer and he needs to read them. Isn't that right?"

"Like I say, we been working on a book together. I been providing the raw materials."

Magoon suspected he'd opened a door for his adversary and led Pinette off to other topics, but the damage had been done. When Warwick cross-examined the old lumberjack, he went straight through the opening. "Mr. Pinette, you say *you* gave ideas to Mr. Bramhall?"

"Lots of them."

"Did he ever say he'd pay you for your ideas? Did he ever say he'd give you your rightful share of an idea if he used it?"

"Never did," said Pinette. "Of course we never got to writing—"

"I see," said Warwick, his voice suggesting that Bramhall was planning to swindle Pinette of his ideas. "Thank you, Mr. Pinette, that will be all."

Vinal Pinette stepped down, and Magoon called Professor Alfred Settlemire to the stand. As the bear watched the lawyers, he practiced a few small arm movements and mouthed some legal sentences of his own. *Could you please tell the jury . . . Objection, your honor . . . Thank you, that will be all . . .*

"Sir," said Magoon to Settlemire, "you are a professor at the University of Maine, is that correct?"

"Yes."

"And Arthur Bramhall was your colleague?"

"Yes."

Magoon pointed toward his client. "Is that Arthur Bramhall?"

"Yes," said Settlemire. "He's—changed though, since he was at the university."

"I'm sure he has, seeing how his life's work was stolen from him. Now, Professor Settlemire, did you ever see Arthur Bramhall's manuscript?"

"Yes, I did. I saw a few chapters."

"You saw a few chapters of the manuscript? You saw them on paper, typewritten?"

"Yes, I did."

"You saw Arthur Bramhall's novel in manuscript form? You're under oath, sir."

"I saw the novel."

"No further questions."

John Warwick approached Professor Settlemire. "Professor, could you tell us in a general way what the contents of this novel were?"

"It was a copy of a best-seller."

"A copy of a best-seller? Why, that's very interesting. I've just heard that Arthur Bramhall used an old lumberjack's stories without sharing with him—"

"Objection!"

"Overruled."

"—and now I hear that he copied a best-seller. We have a word for that, Professor. It's called plagiarism."

"Objection!"

"Overruled."

"What was the title of that best-seller, do you recall?"

"Don't, Mr. Drummond."

"Your colleague made a copy of *Don't, Mr. Drummond?"*

"He copied the style. I didn't think it was a good idea."

"I agree with you, Professor. It's not a good idea. It's an idea that can lead to a great many complications. But let's return to the idea, whether it's good or not. You say Arthur Bramhall plagiarized—excuse me, I mean copied—*Don't, Mr. Drummond*. Have you read that book, Professor?"

"I've glanced at it."

"Could you characterize it for us?"

"It's a piece of romantic trash."

"And you are, one could say, an authority in such matters."

"One would like to think so."

"You like your students to read only the best, I'm sure."

"That's correct."

"Would it interest you to know, Professor, that my client's book, *Destiny and Desire*, is already required reading in hundreds of English classes around the country? That it has received critical acclaim from such authorities in the field as Kenneth Penrod of Columbia University and Samuel Ramsbotham of New York University, two of the most distinguished places of learning in America? Would you say that this is a powerful endorsement of the book's merit?"

"Yes, I'd have to say so. Although Ramsbotham's views on some things—"

"The point is, Professor, my client hasn't written a copy of *Don't, Mr. Drummond*, he's written a highly original work, beloved by the American public and endorsed by two of the greatest minds in the field of contemporary American literature. That doesn't sound anything like the manuscript your colleague showed to you, does it?"

"No," admitted Settlemire uncomfortably, for he'd hoped, in his peculiar way, to have done Bramhall some good here today. He couldn't remember a word of Bramhall's book, nor of *Don't, Mr. Drummond,* for the cells of his memory were stuffed with *as ifs.*

"Professor, when did you see the portion of the novel your colleague showed you?"

"It must've been a year and a half ago."

"And what happened to that novel subsequently?"

"Bramhall had a fire. The novel burned."

"The novel burned? How unfortunate. Yet a year and a half later, your colleague enters this courtroom and claims someone *stole* his novel. Which was it, burned or stolen?" Warwick sent a sidelong glance toward the jury.

"Well," said Settlemire, "Bramhall said it was burned and then stolen."

"Burned *and* stolen?" Warwick looked at the jury again. "This manuscript of his has certainly undergone a harsh fate."

"He rewrote it," said Settlemire. "And then it was stolen." Settlemire's head cocked itself in a strange, sideways manner, rather like a mother baboon looking for fleas; a man who spends his best hours looking for *as ifs* must expect this.

"He rewrote it and *then* it was stolen," said Warwick in tones suggesting the ludicrousness of this idea, while all the time the bear was mimicking his lawyer's gestures. It's not difficult, really, he said to himself. You have to turn your head toward the jury and give them a big smile. You have to stab the air with your paw, then wave it in their faces a little in case they didn't see it.

A passing breeze tucked in at the window and slipped up his nose with scents of the nearby riverbank, of forget-me-nots, golden bells, water hemlocks. He inhaled deeply, closed his eyes, and swayed in his chair. It was springtime in Maine, spring at its most beautiful. With a cry of jubilation, he rolled off his chair onto the floor and writhed around, scratching his back.

"Order in the court!" Judge Spurr's gavel came down with a loud crack. "Counsel, control that man!"

"Hal, for god's sake—" Warwick dropped to his knees beside his client and gave him a vigorous shake.

The bear opened his eyes and drew back his upper lip with a snarl. Judge Spurr brought his gavel down a second time. "Mr. Warwick, if you can't restrain your client, I'm going to hold him in contempt."

"Your honor, I believe he's having some kind of seizure."

"He looks remarkably like a man who's scratching his back."

Warwick took the carafe of water from his table and poured it on the bear, who let out an angry roar. Warwick drew back in fear and turned to the judge. "Your honor, my client is ill."

"He does not appear ill to me, sir. He appears drunk and disorderly and I won't have it."

The jurors were leaning forward in their chairs, and Judge Spurr had risen from his, gavel in hand. Warwick knew that if it came down again it would be with a contempt citation. All of the sympathy they'd gained from judge and jury was going out the window. At that moment, Vinal Pinette's dog, locked in Pinette's truck outside the courtroom, decided he'd been left in the truck long enough and began to bark. He liked to project his bark as far as it would go, for the beauty of the thing. His barking reached the bear's ear and the bear sat up, fully alert.

"Hal," said Warwick, "are you all right?"

The bear's nose was twitching with concern. Had they set their dogs after him? A few more sniffs convinced him the dog was alone and too far away to be a threat. He allowed Warwick to help him back into his chair, where he sat quietly sniffing the air.

Warwick turned toward the judge's bench. "Your honor, Lord Overlook's family has had, for some generations, a rare neurological condition. This episode we've just witnessed is characteristic of the disease."

"Runs in the family, does it?" Judge Spurr was already regretting having spoken so harshly to a lord of the realm. Eccentricity in the aristocracy was something you had to tolerate; the illustrious Overlook line must have thinned a little with inbreeding and produced the weakness he'd just witnessed. Judge Spurr was inclined to be tolerant, as he felt the Overlook family would appreciate such concern. "Is he well enough to continue? If you'd like to move for a recess—"

"We would, your honor."

"This court will recess until tomorrow," said Judge Spurr, and rose from his bench.

Warwick nodded to Magoon, indicating he wanted to talk to him outside the courtroom. The two men retired to a cloakroom and stood together beside an open window looking down into town. Warwick said, "Even though I know we're going to win this case, for the sake of my client's health, we're ready to settle out of court."

Magoon sat with his client in the diner on Main Street. The sound of the river could be heard from their table, along with the cries of a pair of ospreys circling overhead, looking for the glitter of a fish beneath the water. "Cavendish Press is offering us a half a million dollars."

"But they keep the rights? I wouldn't be the author?"

"That's right, Arthur. But your financial problems would be over for the rest of your life."

Arthur Bramhall ran a hand over his tortured, shaggy brow. He heard the cry of the osprey, and he understood its high-pitched sound. He felt the living presence of the river calling him to flow with it.

"Half a million, wisely invested . . ." said Magoon.

"I'm not giving them my book."

"Don't be a fool. The jury's already against us."

"I don't care," growled Bramhall. "I'm the author, and we're going to prove it."

"I no longer know if I can do that."

"The answer is no."

"This is a terrible mistake. Warwick's going to tear you apart on the witness stand."

"I'll tear *him* apart," said Bramhall with a savage growl.

Magoon moved back in his seat, startled by the animal ferocity in his client's eyes.

Vinal Pinette sat with his dog in front of his kitchen stove. "I let him down," said the old man, staring at the scarred wooden floor.

The dog looked up, hoping for a hunk of wiener to find its way to his patient snout. The boss tossed him a few every night around this time.

"I got all tangled up, y'see. That lawyer feller started 'sinuating things, and I went after it, like you after this wiener." Pinette tossed one and the dog grabbed it midair with a fast snap of his jaws and swallowed it whole, as was his custom so no other dog could steal it from him, though there were no other dogs anywhere near, but it paid not to take any chances in the matter of wieners.

"I made Art Bramhall look like a crook, is what I done." The old man's head sank lower as he shook it slowly back and forth. " 'Cause I ain't got no more sense than this here wiener." He shook the end of the wiener in the air, and the dog's head went up and down.

"I'd like to go back in that there courtroom and set it right, but they got all the use out of me they need." Pinette tossed the wiener, and the dog's head made a quick sweep sideways, catching the object and sending it to his stomach in one gulp.

"We ain't never gonna get our book wrote now," said Pinette sadly. The dog retired to his rug behind the stove for some moderate ball-washing. Literature was not one of his burning interests. *The Life of a Wiener*, yes, that might hold his attention, if it was boldly illustrated.

On the following day in court, Eaton Magoon gave proof of his client's literary abilities, from his Ph.D. through the many scholarly essays he'd published in his academic years.

Warwick held up the jacket of *Destiny and Desire* and flourished numerous magazine and newspaper articles about his client. There was no need for him to show anything else, nor could he have if he wanted to, because there was nothing else.

The bear was gesturing in imitation of his lawyer. As Warwick talked, the bear mouthed the words. He'd practiced in his room last night and now he felt he had the pattern down. When Warwick returned to their table, the bear pointed at the witness box and said in a rough whisper, *"Put me up there."*

"No," said Warwick.

The bear's paw closed on Warwick's knee, and a gusher of pain ran up the oil lawyer's leg. He stood and said, "Your honor, I'd like to call my client to the witness box."

The bear was sworn in. He took his oath with great solemnity, his right paw in the air.

He could feel the bright, bubbling words pooling up in him, ready to burst out in a colorful stream.

Warwick didn't leave the area of his desk. "Is your name Hal Jam?"

"Yes."

"Did you write *Destiny and Desire?*"

"Yes."

"No further questions."

The bear looked at Warwick, a hurt expression on his face. "I've got more to say." He gestured like a lawyer toward the jury box.

"You can say it to me," said Magoon as he approached the witness box. "What kind of person are you, Jam?"

"I'm a person," said the bear quickly, glad that this key point had been addressed before anything else. If he was a person, they couldn't put him in a zoo.

"I asked what *kind* of person are you? What kind of person is it, Mr. Jam, who steals another man's hard-won work?"

The bear made the little gesture he'd been practicing, and it felt just like the gestures he'd been watching his lawyer make, but the words that were supposed to accompany it failed to come out. They were swirling around inside him like sparkling fish in a stream but when he tried to pull one from the stream it wriggled through his grasp and slipped away. He turned to the window and sniffed at the air, filling his nose with the scent of the countryside.

Magoon was only inches from him now. "You stole Arthur Bramhall's book. That's who you are, sir. You're a thief, plain and simple. What else can we call you?"

"The fields," said the bear.

"Excuse me?"

"The river," said the bear. "The flowers." He looked toward the courtroom window. His confidence had vanished like a soap bubble. He was thinking of the river, and the pine forest beyond it. He couldn't speak like a lawyer, couldn't make the bright, bubbling sounds that were the true mark of a real person. "The springtime," he said in desperation. "The new buds."

That's the feeling of *Destiny and Desire*, thought one of the jurors to herself as she leaned forward to listen more closely. She'd read the book with much enjoyment and *that*, she said, is the sound of it. She looked at the person in the witness box and knew he was the author of the book she'd loved.

"Is that your answer, sir?" asked Magoon, pressing his advantage. "You're the springtime? You're the new buds?"

"I'm a bear," admitted the crestfallen beast.

Yes, thought the juror, he's the voice of Maine—the

bears, the moose, the birds, the flowers, the trees, and the forest in spring.

"You say you're a bear?" asked Magoon snidely.

"He *is* a bear!" Arthur Bramhall came to his feet, everything clear to him now. "He's the bear who stole my book!"

"Ladies and gentlemen of the jury, have you reached a verdict?"

"We have, your honor."

The jury decision was that the bear was the author of *Destiny and Desire*. All rights in the property, past and present, remained his. They didn't know he was a bear, in spite of his having told them. This was because they were human beings.

At the announcement of the decision, Arthur Bramhall emitted a sound that was guttural and harsh. The members of the jury took this as further confirmation of the correctness of their judgment. A man capable of such a noise could never have written *Destiny and Desire*. They watched him shuffle slowly to the courtroom door, his body swaying from side to side in his badly fitting J. C. Penney suit, which had ripped up the back seam. He gave the door a shove; it flew open and struck the wall with a bang, and he shuffled through, the courtroom deputy watching him suspiciously. The fur-bearing woman, who'd been sending him positive vibrations throughout the trial, now tried to encircle him with clear white light, but he pushed past her with a groan. He went down the stairs and through the lobby to the parking lot, where Vinal Pinette's dog started barking at him, the dog throwing itself against the window of the truck in which it was confined; that sucker is a bear, thought the dog, or I'm not man's best friend.

Arthur Bramhall sat by the edge of a stream. Events from the courtroom were behind him now; he'd been able to sustain an interest in them only while his rage was fresh. But rage had died the moment he set foot back in the forest, and as the days went by, his peace of mind returned. The voice of the forest had his full attention once again. With the passing of weeks, his sense of smell became acute. A network of information became available to him, and he pursued it rapturously, sniffing his way through a layer of experience that had been sealed off from mankind for eons. The fragrant carpets of moss spoke intimately to him, as did the flowers, the pine needles, and wild grasses. The forest was hung with aromatic veils, creating numerous subtle chambers, through which he walked like a sultan in an enchanted palace.

His energy increased. When he ran, he glided, his feet striking lightly, knowing the terrain already. He fed on fish, wild plants, and berries. He needed nothing from anyone.

This is all I ever want, he thought as he sat by the water, looking at the forget-me-nots, the golden bells, the water hemlocks. Their scent was in his nose along with the cool moisture from the stream, which spoke of the miles of country it had crossed. He dipped a hand into the water and smiled at the sparkling drops that collected on his knuckles. He broke into a joyous dance, throwing his powerful arms into the air and stamping his feet.

Vinal Pinette stood watching from an adjacent hill-top. He missed Bramhall's company, but he knew happiness when he saw it, and what more could you want for a friend?

The old woodsman stepped back into the trees and started back through the forest toward home. His watery old eyes glistened as he walked. There was only the sound of his boots moving softly on the forest floor.

"Hal, I'm so very glad to finally have the chance to meet you," said the vice president, on the south lawn of the White House.

The bear sniffed the vice president, going past the aftershave to the essential scent and trying to place where he'd smelled it last. I've met this dominant male before, he thought to himself.

Shaking the bear's hand, the vice president said, "I owe you a great deal."

"I bopped him on the head!" said the bear, suddenly remembering the hotel lobby where he'd settled a territorial claim.

"You certainly did bop him on the head," said the vice president. "You're a genuine American hero, Hal."

"*Ursus americanus,*" said the bear, nodding.

The vice president allowed himself a momentary frown of puzzlement, but the bear did not elaborate. He was sniffing the warm scent of the flowers that greeted them as they entered the president's private garden. There's some excellent honey around these parts, or I'm not Hal Jam.

"The president wants to meet you too. He'll be along in a minute."

"Who's he?" asked the bear.

Again, the vice president frowned, and began to understand why, at the briefing for this meeting, he'd been told that Hal Jam was odd. "My wife read your book. She'd like you to sign it for her."

"I can sign my name," said the bear. "Hal Jam. I'm a person."

The vice president, maintaining his puzzled frown, continued in step with his guest, in the informal stroll advised by his staff. Hal Jam was known for celebrating nature in his work, and the vice president's staff had decided he could be counted as an environmentalist. The presidential garden, therefore, seemed the most appropriate setting in which to say thank you to him. It was felt that Jam was probably a moderate, though there'd been talk that he might be tilting toward the far right, indicated by his meeting with the Reverend Norbert Sinkler, and the president did not want to lose another influential intellectual. So, though Hal Jam was proving to be peculiar, the vice president was disposed to be patient, and to plumb the depths of his potentially helpful guest.

"I understand that you're from Maine," said the vice president. "We've fought hard to preserve the wilderness there."

"I prefer hotels," said the bear. "They wash your underwear."

The vice president smiled, feeling it was best to smile, as a photo op would be coming up, and he didn't want to be frowning at the man who'd saved him from being exploded all over the lobby of the Ritz Carlton. But he knew he was far from plumbing the depths of Hal Jam.

"Do you like room service?" asked the bear.

"It's all right," said the vice president, trying to stay light.

"There's no room service in the woods," said the bear, nodding sagely as he dispensed this valuable information.

"Here comes the president," said the vice president with relief, as Secret Service agents appeared at the west corner of the Executive Mansion. "We'll be meeting him, and then there'll be a luncheon with a number of people from the arts. I'm sure you'll be seeing folks you know."

The bear sniffed the air, trying to pick up the cooking smells from the White House. "Have you got candidacy on the menu?"

"Glad you asked. Because we'd like your help."

The president came toward them, hand outstretched, smiling. "Mr. Jam, I sure am proud to meet you."

The bear noted that all the other males were showing deference to this one. Must have kicked a lot of ass, reflected the bear.

The president did all the talking as they walked. The bear didn't understand anything that was said, which was fine. Sometimes when he tried to understand human beings he got into trouble.

They entered through the south side of the building, Secret Service agents moving ahead of them. The president said, "We're going to have our luncheon in the Green Room today."

"I bet it isn't green," said the bear knowledgeably.

Across the president's brow passed the same puzzled frown which had ruffled the vice-presidential forehead. "Yes, it is. The walls are green silk, and the drapes match. Mrs. Kennedy did the redecorating herself."

The bear didn't know who Mrs. Kennedy was. But he was glad she knew enough to make the Green Room green.

"I hope you won't be a stranger here at the White House, Hal," said the president as he prepared to fork away to other matters. Lowering his voice, he said, "The far right is mobilized, Hal. The fight is tougher than ever. I hope your next book will treat us as fairly as the last one did."

"No problem."

"Thank you, Hal," said the president, and gave an almost imperceptible nod of satisfaction to the vice president.

"I change my underwear every day," said the bear,

just to keep things friendly, at which point he was quickly handed over to a staff member. He followed her to the Green Room, which was filling with guests from the world of arts and letters. Eunice Cotton was there, as her angel books were popular in Washington; angels were felt to be politically neutral and gave a gloss of piety without committing anyone on Capitol Hill to anything too muscularly Christian.

"Here you are!" cried Eunice, rushing toward the bear. "There's someone I'm dying for you to meet. He's a saint."

Eunice conducted them toward a frail old man standing by himself in a corner of the Green Room. "He's been in a Cuban jail for almost thirty years," explained Eunice under her breath. "Castro just let him go. Senator Loveman was telling me all about it."

The old man extended a shaking hand to the bear and smiled vaguely at Eunice. His English was perfect—he'd been educated at Eton and had spent much of his life at Oxford, where he'd produced his abstruse philosophical works—but his voice was thin and weak. Castro's prison had broken him; deep creases marked his mouth and eyes, and the skin was stretched tight to his skull. "Delighted to meet you," he said, but his focus was on a far-off place. Eunice sensed he was seeing the angelic plane which awaited him in the not-too-distant future. But in fact he was thinking of the companion with whom he'd shared his last years in prison, a rat of whom he'd grown terribly fond. Ratty would have enjoyed this banquet, thought the old man to himself. Such a lot of food.

"It's a thrill for me to bring you two together," said Eunice. "My two living angels."

The old man listened to Eunice politely, but Ratty was on his mind. The dear little chap would have had such fun nibbling at everything today. I'd have to caution him to go slow, wouldn't I, or he'd overeat and bloat himself.

"I don't know much about philosophy," admitted Eunice, "though of course my heavenly angels do."

"How charming," said the old man with a senile smile. Apparently he'd been an important philosopher, everyone said so, but Ratty was the philosophical one. Now, there was a brilliant mind.

"At times when you were in jail," said Eunice, "you must have thought the whole world had forgotten your existence."

The old man listened, in a silvery fog. After his first years of imprisonment, his philosophy had failed him, and he'd escaped grim reality by writing a fantasy, furtively, on scraps of toilet paper. It became his central focus, a work not of political revolution, but of love, a romantic story he'd set in New England, a place he'd visited only once, before returning to the wretched island of his birth, where he'd fallen foul of Castro. Because his glimpse of New

England had been so brief, it shone brightly in the novel. Having been deprived of female company, he'd created a heroine of great beauty and sensitivity, who then inhabited the imaginative spaces of his soul, helping him to cope with his overwhelming solitude and deprivation. Even so, he finally succumbed to the rigors of prison life, to maltreatment, poor diet, fever, parasites. On the day he finished his novel, he'd begun his relationship with Ratty. Oh, thought the old man, if only Ratty were here today, how much pleasure it would give me.

"We know you haven't had much time to adjust to freedom," said Eunice sympathetically, "the way they whisked you right up here to Washington. But Senator Loveland's committee is hoping that your presence will be a rallying point for freeing other political prisoners around the world."

It seemed to the old man that it was only yesterday that he'd walked out of prison with his novel under his arm. It was under his arm now, in a battered leather briefcase. No one knew of its existence, only he, and now he hardly knew what it contained—something about love—or was it about Ratty? He hoped it was about Ratty.

The old philosopher gazed around the room. Such excitement, so many people. It was really too much, he felt quite weak. There was a peculiar bubbling in his chest . . . a fountain was erupting.

"Oh! . . . oh dear . . . catch him, Hal! Quick, a doctor!"

The bear gently carried the little old man through the crowd and laid him down on a couch. A doctor was there in moments, took the old man's pulse, and shook his head.

The bear backed up slowly through the craning figures in the crowd. Once outside the Green Room, he hurried down the hall. The guards, recognizing him as the president's personal guest, nodded to him as he passed.

He stepped out of the White House and was met by the Secret Service agent who'd been with the vice president in Boston. "Hey, how're you doing?" asked the agent with a grin, and made the gesture of bopping someone on the head.

"Fine," said the bear, and signaled for his limousine. The signal was relayed to the VIP holding area, and his limo was brought forward. He ducked into the backseat, and there, behind the tinted windows, he breathed a sigh of relief.

"Yessir," said the driver. "Where to?"

"New York City," said the bear.

"New York City?"

"Do you know where it is?"

"No problem."

The limo pulled out onto E Street, and the bear opened the battered leather briefcase.

There, inside, on fragile, wrinkled squares of paper, in the crabbed, spidery hand of one who writes by night, surreptitiously, was everything a bear needed for his much-awaited sequel.

He reached into the limo's bar, which had been stocked according to his special instructions. He removed a jar of honey and put it to his lips.

Wild blueberry. You can't beat that.

He opened a bag of Cheesy Things and settled back into the seat for the long ride home.

William Kotzwinkle is the author of such enduring classics as *The Fan Man, Doctor Rat, Swimmer in the Secret Sea, Fata Morgana*, and *E.T.: The Extraterrestrial*. His most recent novel, *The Game of Thirty*, was hailed by Stephen King as "top level entertainment . . . a suspense novel to rank with classics of the genre." Mr. Kotzwinkle lives with his wife, writer Elizabeth Gundy, on an island off the Maine coast.